MORE PRAISE FOR QUIET AS TH_

"This deeply moving collection of stories hums and glows with the interconnected lives of an extended immigrant family from Vietnam. Chau navigates her characters' lives—their tragedy and humor, longings and furies, vast losses and secret beauties—with grace, skill, and ferocious compassion. *Quiet As They Come* announces the arrival of an astonishing literary talent with a great deal to say about the intricacies of family life, coming of age, emigration, and—above all—the treasures buried in the human heart."
—Carolina De Robertis, *The Invisible Mountain*

"What a rich and charming collection of stories this is. It offers an insider's view of the immigrant experience: a world divided, one culture from another, past from present, parent from child."
—Lynn Freed, *The Curse of the Appropriate Man*

"In stories that manage to be both playful and poignant, Angie Chau displays her exceptional gift for capturing the intricate interactions between parents and children, men and women, and Vietnamese and American cultures. There's grit beneath the sparkle of her language. Chau's intimate portrayal of characters who must navigate the uncertain terrain between what's left behind and what lies ahead is revelatory." —Leslie Larson, *Breaking Out of Bedlam*

"Chau's characters bristle with life. They're full of beauty and grit, love and cowardice, bravery and spite. Many of them are new to this country, and Chau's gift for detailed observation made me see San Francisco again as though it were new to me. Gosh, this book practically has a heartbeat. A rare gift, indeed."—Robin Romm, *The Mercy Papers*

QUIET
AS THEY
COME

QUIET
AS THEY
COME

ANGIE CHAU

ig
PUBLISHING

BROOKLYN, NEW YORK

Printed in the United States of America
10 9 8 7 6 5 4 3 2

Ig Publishing
392 Clinton Avenue
Brooklyn, NY 11238
www.igpub.com

Library of Congress Cataloging-in-Publication Data

Chau, Angie.
 Quiet as they come / Angie Chau.
    p. cm.
 ISBN 978-1-935439-18-9 (alk. paper)
 1. Vietnamese Americans--Fiction. 2. Refugees--Fiction. 3. San
Francisco (Calif.)--Fiction. 4. Domestic fiction. [1. California--
History--1950---Fiction.] I. Title.
 PS3603.H38Q85 2010
 813'.6--dc22
                                    2010023043

For my parents

CONTENTS

Longing, we say, because desire is full
of endless distances.

—Robert Hass, *Meditation at Lagunitas*

HUNGER

I live in a three-bedroom house with my mom and dad and little sister Michelle. We have the corner bedroom because my mom can't sleep. Down the hall, the biggest bedroom goes to my uncle and aunt because they have three sons. The smallest room goes to my aunt Kim because it's only her and Sophia and Marcel who don't have a dad.

The house is big and old. There are lots of hidden closets and corners and secrets inside. Like how we're not allowed to bring up Uncle Duc because he's in jail in Vietnam. Or how we have to step over my dad when we go to the bathroom at night, but come morning we have to pretend he was never sleeping in the hallway. Or how we're not supposed to hear Uncle Lam's fists on Aunt Trang's body. So when it's the Fourth of July, and all our parents leave so they can work over-time, and they close all the curtains because they say it'll keep the house cooler, I wonder if it's to keep us a secret too.

It is dark inside the house because everything is wood and the windows are covered. It is loud because the boys are banging on the pots. It is hot because it's the holiday that has to be warm enough for families to sit and watch fireworks in the night. I sit with a radio in the shadows of the living room floor. My name is Elle. It's not my real name. That's kind of a secret too.

No one at school knows it's my fake name. My parents changed it so I would fit better. Sometimes I wonder if they'll change my last name too. And if they do, what will become of the old me? The Vietnamese name with the two letters that match like your favorite pair of socks.

Everyone else got famous people names like Sophia Loren and Marcel, short for Marcello Mastroianni. The three boys are named after the Rat Pack, Uncle Lam's favorite group. When I ask my mom why I didn't get a cool famous name, she looks around to make sure nobody else is around and whispers, "I would never do that to you. It's like announcing you still have salt behind your ears."

My mom talks in riddles and poems. It's her way of saying she doesn't want everyone to know that we only arrived in America five months ago. It means she wouldn't want the world to know that we had to escape here by boat. The way she talks and puts words together is different from the other adults. Maybe it's because she studied theater when she was young. She can make you feel like you are the sun or just as quickly a speck of dirt. When she talks everyone snaps to attention. But maybe they just can't help but look at her she is that beautiful. Everyone says she would have been a famous actress in Vietnam if we hadn't left. I can imagine her name in lights.

If my parents want to change my last name, I will say, *please*, if I'm good can I choose it this time? And then I will say, doesn't Estrada sound nice? And then they'll think it's because I'm in love with Erik Estrada. But really it's because I'd have two Es for Elle Estrada the way I used to have two Ts for Thao Tran.

Erik Estrada is my favorite actor. I wear a shirt with him flat across my heart. I wear it every day until my mom peels it off and says, "Dirty girl, you should have been born a boy."

The shirt has strings that tie behind my neck. It's yellow, my favorite color because it looks like sunshine. The iron-on says *Chips* and he's sitting on a motorcycle. He cradles his helmet in his arm like a baby. His shades are off so you can see his soft brown eyes. He has big white teeth and wavy black hair. He's a policeman. Nobody would mess with me if we were together.

The man on the radio says, "San Francisco put away your frying pans. It's so hot today you can cook an egg on the pavement!"

Sophia says, "I want eggs. I'm hungry."

I say, "I wish we were still at the refugee camp."

Frank, Dean, and Sammie in descending order watch from the sofa like monkeys in a banyan tree. Frank, the oldest, rolls his eyes and says, "That's lame. You'd be dead if you were still there." He is ten and only two years older than me but he acts like he's already grown.

I say, "At least we went swimming there."

In Malaysia, my dad would take all the kids to a swimming hole made entirely of black shells. He taught us how to swim. He taught us how to dig for clams. He taught us times tables. My dad's a good teacher because he used to be one. One day, he taught us how to make paper kites out of yesterday's newspaper and spoiled white rice for glue. The adults cheered when they saw the kite tails flapping in the wind. They said it looked like freedom.

The little kids jump up and down on the hardwood floors and raise their hands in the air. "I want to go swimming," they say. "Me too, yay, me three!"

The boys pull the sofa-bed away from the wall and throw the cushions to the floor. Between the mattress folds and tangled sheets there are coins disguised as dust balls. The girls look in the kitchen. We find a lonely nickel behind the refrigerator. It's no surprise. There's never anything in our kitchen except the piled up government cartons of powdered milk and canned meats that our parents don't know how to eat.

Frank is the oldest boy of the oldest man in the house so he gets to be the boss. He makes all of us sit in a straight line on the floor. We have to report what we put into the community pot. But when we get to Marcel, he just shrugs his shoulders.

Franks says, "You little cheap skate, you're going into the phone booth."

Marcel shoves his shiny red lock box under his t-shirt. His belly jingles filled with the coins.

Frank says, "Hand over your money or you're going in." He eyes the chipped paint of the closet door. Frank is like his father. He's tall and handsome. He can be kind or cruel.

The hallway closet is called the phone booth because it has the magical power of transformation. Like when Superman goes inside and changes from a nerdy journalist into a superhero. Our parents keep their shared interview clothes in there. They go in looking fresh off the boat and come out looking like shiny Americans of the future. They don't mind the smell of mothballs mixed with each other's faded imposter cologne. They think it will bring them closer to the American Dream. On an interview day, they put on these costumes bought on layaway from Sears, and fly off with Mercedes dreams gleaming in their eyes like stars.

The phone booth is also where we go when we get punished. We have to kneel in the dark until our parents let us out. Uncle Lam makes the boys kneel on rice grains. Sometimes they're in there until their knees bleed. My dad says it's not right. My mom says it's none of our business. I say the stink in there is bad enough.

Marcel says, "But I'm saving for when my dad comes."

Frank says, "You're a liar. You don't have a dad. You're a bastard."

Sophia screams, "We do too have a dad!"

Sammie copies his older brother and chants, "You don't have a *da-ad*. You don't have a *daad*. You're a *bass-turd*."

Sophia starts crying. Marcel who is protective of his little sister grabs a fierce fistful of Sammie's hair and yanks it.

Dean says, "Let go of my little brother," and punches Marcel in the back.

Sophia kicks Dean in the shin. Frank pushes her off.

It's the Rat Pack against the Italian movie stars and I don't know where to look or what to do so I count the money. "Stop it! Stop it! Look, we have enough."

Frank says, "Yeah, right. You're just a girl. You don't know how to do math."

"Then you stay home smarty pants." I stand up with my hand on my hip. I swivel and arch my back the way they do it in the Sergio Valente commercial. My sister Michelle and I have been practicing in front of the mirror. We flip our hair, swing our heads, and say, "We love you Sergio!" I stick my butt out and turn to them and and say, "I don't know about you guys but I'm taking the clean towel." Michelle who always copies me does the same and follows down the long dark hallway.

Outside, it's so hot it feels like our eyelashes will get charred. The Avenues are empty. We live in the Sunset District where rows and rows of attached houses line the streets like soldiers, shoulder to shoulder, in waiting. Every now and then a car passes with floats and hula hoops and colored umbrellas poking out the windows like a carnival. I picture them going to the beach, playing tag, catching the sea breeze. They're having a picnic. They're eating fried chicken, and potato salad, and if they're really lucky maybe their mom even made lettuce wraps with shrimp.

We are a family of dark-haired pigeons. We flit in the heat

of the city streets, pecking at nothing but crumbs and cement. Frank is wearing his new black shades from Woolsworth's and tries to keep a cool distance. He swaggers ahead, with his feathered hair and a comb sticking out of his back pocket. Behind him Dean and Marcel are buddies again. They kick at crumpled soda cans glinting in the gutter. Michelle chases after them. The little ones, Sophia and Sammie, waddle like ducks with orange floaties strapped to their arms. I anchor the flock.

They're chirping, "Are we there yet?"

They're twittering, "How much longer?"

They squawk, "It's so hot. It's so hot. It's so hot."

I say, "Don't be such babies." The sweat streams down my chest. I pull out my collar and blow down. Frank stops to watch.

He says, "Look, what a perv, she's trying to check herself out." The little kids laugh because they don't know any better. Dean and Marcel are old enough to blush and turn away.

On Quintara Ave., there's an old white man watering his plants. He's wearing plaid shorts and a blue fishing hat and he's the only person we've seen outside all day. Frank says, "Check out Humpty-Dumpty," because the man is round as a ball. When we get closer, we see that his plants and bushes are shaped like animals. We gasp because it's as if we've walked into a zoo. "How cool," I say because it's beautiful. The boys say, "That's bad, blood," because they want to sound tough.

At the man's knees, the bush is in the shape of a big turtle. It has a leafless twig for a tail. The green hose sprays water on the turtle's shell. There is also a bear, a dog, and a bunny! Little Sophia reaches for the pointy ears. It's dotted with pretty purple flowers. I say, "Don't even try."

I don't think he wants us kids to bother him until he turns, raises the sprayer to the sky, and showers us. We giggle beneath the umbrella of sprinkles. Above us, a rainbow stretches across the curtain of mist. We stand still, side by side, single file like we've been taught at school. "More, me more," each one says because nobody wants to get passed up. He directs the water from left to right, back and forth. It rains down on us in big refreshing drops, splattering our faces. I open my mouth and soon the younger ones do the same. We chirp with our begging beaks lifted to the skies. And while we laugh with our throats bared and our eyes squinting against the sun, he lowers the nozzle and aims directly at our bodies. He presses the handle all the way. The water sprays an angry blast.

"Stop it," I say, "it hurts." After this, he aims only at me. The blast stings like being slapped again and again. The water pushes me off the curb.

"Sneaky rats, my brother marched at Bataan," he says. I drink water and choke for air. My hair gags me. "C'mon ya dirty Japs, I'm goin' wash you up." The man is cursing so hard he's spitting.

I turn my back and curl into a snail with my knees on the ground. The blast pounds my spine. It unravels the ribbon of my shirt. I wrap my arms around my chest to cover up. My cousins stand frozen until I yell, "Help!"

Frank grabs a chalk rock from the man's rock garden and pegs him in the stomach. The man folds over and we all run. I am running and my shirt has fallen but I don't care. From half a block away I throw a rock aiming at his head. It grazes his blue fishing hat and clangs off his garage door. He's tugging the eagle wings of his belt buckle. It's cinched so high, the eagle soars toward his chest. His other hand is waving above his head, beckoning, daring us to return.

Frank says, "If you'd hit him you would have really been busted."

I pull my shirt up and say, "I don't care."

While Frank ties the bow in back for me he says, "Girl, you'd be sent back to Nam."

I say, "If I'm lucky." There's another chalk rock in my hand. I clutch it so tight it digs dent marks in my fist. I throw it on the ground and watch it break into little pieces.

I want to cry. But I can't. I know that if I cry, the kids will cry too and I can't let that man beat us. Make us look stupid, so that everyone would see us, dripping and wet, a bunch of snotty-nosed kids, sorry and parentless, on the Fourth of July.

We walk for two blocks and then little Sophia says, "Hooray, the plane!"

Marcel and Dean point up at the blue sky. Using their Tattoo from *Fantasy Island* nasally voice they say, "Look boss, the *plane*, the *plane*," cracking each other up.

We speed up because seeing the plane means that we're almost at the swimming pool. From a distance, the playground looks like a giant piece of aluminum foil. The silver plane is in the middle of a sawdust box surrounded by slides and swing sets. Everything is so shiny it's blinding. I think we'll burn if we walk closer. The little kids don't care. They run ahead.

I scream after them, "Don't go down the slide. It'll burn the back of your legs." Then I turn to Frank and ask, "What's a Jap anyway?"

He says, "It means Japanese, duh! Why?"

"That's what the man called us, remember? Japs. Dirty Japs. We're not even Japanese."

Frank says, "I know, but we all look the same to them."

I don't say anything. I have to think about what it means.

Frank puts his arm around me. He says, "Don't worry about it. Humpty Dumpty was just a jerk." He's walking beside me so close I can hear his stomach growl. I think he's being a softie because he's hungry until his hand reaches behind my neck and tries to pull at my bow. "Don't you remember? Chinese, Japanese, dirty knees, look at these!" Frank lifts his shirt and flashes his nipples and sticks his tongue out. "Just like yours!" he says.

Frank disappears into the belly of the plane. On its side in faded black letters it says U.S.S. Coral Sea. It could have been a real plane, used in a real war, like the war we came from. I bet the plane hides lots of secrets too.

I don't see the kids but I can hear their muffled voices echoing inside as if they've been swallowed. I yell down the cockpit and bang on the doors. I want them out. I want to see my sister's snaggle tooth, and Marcel's goggle eyes, and Sophia's pout, and Sammie's broom hair, and Dean's furry mole, and Frank with the chin always jutting out like a dare.

"Let's go swimming. C'mon are you ready or not?" I stomp on the wings with both feet jumping up and down. They don't answer. They're shhing each other quiet beneath me. I think of my uncle who my mom said betrayed the family by staying in underground tunnels with the Viet Cong all those years. I yell, "Last one out's a Commie. See ya, wouldn't wanna be ya." I hear the scuttle of footsteps on tin. They sound like a herd of stallions galloping into the light. This works each time. In our family there is nothing worse than being considered a VC.

At the Charlie Sava Swimming Pool, we wait in line behind a busload of kids. They all have matching blue t-shirts that says San Francisco Chinese Baptist Church on them. The boys wear gold crosses and are eating bologna sandwiches. They drink grape sodas and have purple moustaches above their lips. The girls wear gold crosses and Hello Kitty barrettes and tell the boys they're not supposed to eat before they swim. They say, "I heard you'll sink if you eat too much." I feel so weak, I think I'll sink because I've eaten too little.

My mom says that unless we turn into Chinese Baptists, the church sponsors will kick us out of our house with our dark halls, loose door knobs, wobbly chandeliers, and bathroom lines. My mom says she doesn't want to be Baptist and neither do my uncles and aunts, but we have to pretend that we do for as long as we can. I just hope if it happens, I don't have to wear a gold cross. Jewelry gives me a rash.

The line moves as slow as a granny. My little sister is biting the inside of her cheek. Marcel is staring out at the traffic, glassy-eyed. Frank isn't even looking at the Chinese girls anymore. The smell of chlorine and wet towels is making me sick. My stomach feels like there is somebody kicking it from the inside out. I hold it like a watermelon and try to pat it down. When the lady inside the ticket booth says, "You're up, honey," I don't know what to do.

I reach to pay. We can't turn around now. But then five-year- old Sammie whispers something into Frank's ear and starts crying. Sophia sees this and begins to bawl. Frank puts his hand up like a crosswalk guard. He comes to me and says, "The cry babies say they're too hungry to swim." Even though Frank wants to act hard, his stomach rumbles loud as a fog horn, louder than the crying kids. He says, "I guess we should spend the money on food?"

At the bus stop, Dean says, "What a waste!"

Michelle my copycat sister says, "What a shame!"

They don't want to take the bus because if we walk we can save the money for food. It'd be fine except the little ones are holding their bellies and saying they can't walk any further.

Marcel says, "This sucks! Maybe we should split up."

I tell him, "Fine, walk. But you won't get any extra pizza."

Frank backs me up and says, "Yeah, it's still a community pot."

We ride the bus with our eyes looking down. We look at the aisle's ridges and the gum stuck in the ruts. We don't notice the blue skies, or the green leaves, or the smiling flowers everywhere. We only see the oil spills that rise like genies from the streets and think one wish, give me just one.

Inside Big Yo's, it's dark and the lights are off. The pizza parlor feels like outer space because of the blinking video games and flashing beer signs and the ring from the TV with the volume on high. There's a man under the TV and he gets up from his stool. The fan on the counter blows his hair into cotton candy clouds. He says, "What you kids want?" But we don't say anything. "Why aren't ya barbecuing or something with the rest of the masses out there?" He signals toward the open door and squints against the glare of sun streaming in. We all look down at the black and white checkered floors. He says, "Whatever," and goes back to his seat.

He's watching Giants baseball. When he's not in front of the fan his hair settles into waves like the ones in Malaysia. Not too big and not too small but fun enough. He has nice eyes and big white teeth. He asks me, "See something ya like?"

I blush. I can see my face in the mirrored beer sign all red. I can see my goose bumps because I get cold when I'm hungry. I can see my hair flattened against my head, and my soggy shirt with the little triangles poking through, a shy hello, right under where it says *Chips* on my chest.

"Just holler," he says. "It's the bottom of the ninth and we're down by two. But we already have two men on base and only one out." He punches his left palm with his right fist and says, "C'mon now, nice and easy, nice and easy." When he does this, he looks like Erik Estrada.

The kids are hovering around Ms. Pac-Man. They are fighting over who gets to hold on to the joy stick. Frank is sitting with his head on the table. He's not being bossy anymore. He's just holding his stomach with both of his hands. I collect everyone's money. I count the quarters first, then the dimes, then the lonely nickel from behind the fridge, and finally the pennies. I recount it to double check but still we only have enough for exactly one slice of pepperoni. If we had thirty more cents we could have had two cheese slices. If we hadn't taken the bus, we could have gotten one cheese and one pepperoni.

I smash my hair back into place. I borrow Frank's comb. I fluff up my shirt to air it out and tie it in a knot above my belly button. I pinch my cheeks to make them have rosy apples like I've seen mom do. Finally, I take a deep breath before I approach.

I hear the man yell, "Shit! God, damn-it!" before I've reached the counter. Then he says, "Are ya gonna stand there all day or are ya gonna order?"

The coins are all sweaty inside my fist. I can smell the tinny stink of it. I nod.

"All right, then what'll it be?"

I point to the pepperoni behind the glass.

"How many?"

I hold up a finger.

"One? How 'bout your friends there?"

I shake my head no from side to side.

He says, "Not much of a talker huh?"

I'm holding my breath and then I say quick as I can, "Two please, if we can owe you."

He's looking at the TV. I bite my bottom lip and wait. It is only a commercial but he watches closely because there are two pretty women at the beach in red, white, and blue bikinis. Together they smile and say, "This Bud's for you." The game comes back on. He puts a pepperoni slice on a paper plate.

"There ya go, one-fifty," he says. He sits back down with his eyes still glued to the screen.

I put the exact change on the counter beside the register. I wonder if the man didn't hear me or if he was too embarrassed to say no. My shirt looks stupid and I yank it back down.

Sammie runs up and says, "Where's my slice?"

Sophia says, "That's mine."

"Shut-up," I say.

I leave so the man won't be even more embarrassed for us. I pick the booth as far away from him as possible. We gather in the darkest corner of the room. It's as if we've fallen in a well.

"But where's mine?" says Sophia. Her bottom lip sticks out in a pout.

I give her the first bite so she won't cry. We pass the slice around. Each one takes a bite and then watches as the next person takes their bite. We watch each other like tigers, or rats, or Viet Cong spies. We say to each other, "Don't eat it all," or "We're skipping you next time," or "Oink! Oink!"

The seven of us are bent over the one slice. Our elbows are on the table. There are five pieces of pepperoni so we divide them in half to make ten. There are three halves left and those go to the youngest. Our parents always tell us older siblings take care of younger siblings so Frank and I, and Dean and Marcel have to hold out. I see the spit bubble on the corners of Frank's mouth. We are pigs at the trough, another secret to hide.

When we are done we stare at the white paper plate with the wet grease spots. Marcel picks up the paper plate and licks at the yellow-orange trickles of oil. He then puts the plate smack to his face and tries to suck out every last bit of it. We all understand that want. Not one of us makes fun of him for it, for cherishing that extra bit. We watch silently. It's the first time we've been quiet all day.

We are perfectly still, so still that we are surprised when the man finds us and stands over our table. He has a big grin on his face but he says, "Hey kids, you know you're not supposed to be here if you're not eating or playing games." In the dimness, his teeth look bright white. It reminds me of Little Red Riding Hood and the wolf before he eats the little girl. Then the man shrugs his shoulders and says, "Sorry guys, store policy."

We pick up our towels and the orange arm floats and the sunglasses that Frank almost forgets. We're scooting out when the man says, "Hey stop, what do you think you're doing?"

I say, "You told us to leave, so we're going!" After I say it I suck my lips into my mouth and look around at the others hoping he didn't notice it was me.

He tells me, "I never told you to leave. I said you're not supposed to be here."

I'm sure the man's just messing with us now. Frank's eyes are wet. They shine big and then he juts his chin out at me. I swallow the lump in my throat and say, "Well, we don't like it here anyway."

The man says, "Hold on to your horses!"

Frank's eyes widen and he says, "Come on, we better go."

But the tears have gushed out and once I start I can't stop. And I hear myself saying something about Buddha and America and how we don't want to be Japanese Baptists, and how we're going to do good in school and get good grades so we can "Go back to Vietnam."

The man shakes his head in disappointment. He says, "You want to go back to where? What-cha-ma-call-it? Now what kind of thing is that to say on the Fourth of July? What da ya mean you don't like it here? When you're living in the home of the Giants, huh? Would you get food like this anywhere else?" His smile reaches his ears. From behind his back, he sweeps out a big disk glistening with grease and cheese and pepperoni. He says, "How about you guys help me celebrate our whooping Padre butt today, huh?"

All the kids cheer and slide back in the booth. The man pulls up a chair and he sits in it backwards at the head of the table. Everyone is happy to claim their own slice but I'm too ashamed to eat. I put my head on the table and bury my face in my arms until the man taps my shoulder and puts a slice on my napkin. He says close to my ear, "Some day some lucky guy will tell you how cute you are when you get mad." He winks at me. "Come on now, eat up ya little firecracker."

We sit in a darkened booth on the Fourth of July. We eat pizza and listen to baseball. The man tells us how close the game was. He describes the last play. The way Chili Davis hit a double, and Max Venable stole second, and Jeff Ransom slid into home. He says how the stadium roared and everyone jumped out of their seats and the coach was so happy he cried. He says, "That can happen to you. Sometimes you're so happy that you cry." He says it straight at me. He loves baseball so much he makes it sound like a big amusement park, and calls it the Big Show with things like cracker jacks, and circus catches, goose eggs, and curtain calls. And even though we don't get to see fireworks that night because our parents are too tired to take us out, in my sleep, I see balls like comets blazing across the night sky, and stars like lollipops shooting pop flies.

THE PUSSYCATS

It sounded like a purely capitalistic concept when her six-year-old explained it. "You bring something special into class and tell everyone about it." In Vietnam, this was called bragging. In America, it was called Show and Tell. They had arrived in this country only six months ago and already her daughter was begging for things, and of all things, Sophia wanted a cat. The best Kim could offer was a movie called *The Pussycats*. It would be Sophia's first ever outing to a movie theater and Kim hoped movie magic would cure her daughter's meowing.

Although the movie outing was indulgent, she wanted to make it up to Sophia for missing their promised Fourth of July play date. Kim's schedule consisted of ESL class in the mornings, Miss Marty's beauty school in the afternoons, and weekend work at a beauty salon to earn extra cash. This was her first entire weekend off in two months.

She held Sophia's hand as they walked at a brisk pace to the discounted matinee. The sun was out, her heart raced, and Kim felt alive, as if anything was possible on a day like this. When they passed a phone booth she thought, why not call him, poor guy's probably home alone. Kim hopped in and dialed but the longer the rings grew, the more nervous she got. Every succeeding ring became shriller than the one before. The blank spaces in between them were dark pockets to spin inside and cause to hold her breath.

She was unprepared for her foolishness. After all, they'd been friends for decades. She reminded herself that Bao was all alone in this country. She reminded herself that while she had the security of her entire extended family sharing a house with her, he was living in a rented room at the Y. Her rationale gave her the strength to hold on long enough to hear the receptionist say, "Sorry he's out."

Because of the delay, mother and daughter ran the last two blocks to the theater. Kim was disappointed by the look of the place when she arrived out of breath. She checked the newspaper clipping in her purse. She blinked and reread the address a second time. Kim had somehow imagined an American theater to be flashier, with gilt and bright lights, and glossy posters behind shiny glass. Before her was a nondescript brown box of a building. Behind a scratchy plastic panel, a frizzy-haired young man sat reading a paperback.

Kim approached, knocked, and made her hand like a peace sign. He nudged his glasses up the bridge of his nose, squinted and nodded, pushed out the money tray, and returned to his reading.

Inside the darkened theater, her daughter squeezed her hand and said, "I can't see!" It made more peculiar the silence. As they made their way up the aisle she noticed that most moviegoers were sitting alone and at wide intervals. Something simply felt odd. The room smelled sanitized as if it had been doused with a large bucket of bleach. And when she finally took a seat, it was so scratchy it felt as if she were sitting on a pineapple, This final assault reminded Kim of all the ways big and small she kept on blundering in this country. Her once keen judgment seemed constantly off-track. She was about to usher her daughter out when the projector lights flickered on. It illuminated Sophia's black Mary-Janes which had been polished for this very occasion and shined against the glow of the screen. Sophia pointed and said as if already seduced, "Mama . . . it's starting, look."

On screen, half a dozen nurses all slim, young, and pretty, lined up in a row. They wore starched white dresses and little white caps. Their hair was pinned into buns. Their legs were in tan nylons. Each woman would twirl when a man passed by jotting notes. Their dainty feet were all in white round-toed heels. The man in the scene was middle aged and ordinary. He wore a pressed shirt that strained across his midsection. When he reached the end of the line, the girls gathered around the chart, put their hands to their mouths, and erupted into a tide of giggles. Kim fidgeted in her seat. She had always preferred Italian films. Her children were evidence. When counseled to give her children Western names to make their assimilation easier, Kim had renamed Sophia after Sophia Loren and Marcel for Marcello Mastroianni.

Despite her efforts to forge ahead with life, an act as benign as going to the movies made her miss her husband even more. Back in Sàigòn, Kim and Duc used to go to the movies every Friday night. They would get durian shakes and boiled peanuts and as soon as the lights went out, she'd rest her head on his shoulder, inhale his cinnamon smell, and give herself over to the fantasy of the film.

Her favorite American movie was *Cat on a Hot Tin Roof*. She remembered Elizabeth Taylor stunningly hissing for affection. Her favorite scene was when Elizabeth Taylor's character said, "I'm not living with you! We occupy the same cage that's all." In that moment, Kim was so transfixed that she forgot all about the M&M's in her hand. She smashed every single one of the candied shells. Her husband teased her endlessly. She thought that was bad enough but then it got even worse.

Something about Liz Taylor's performance was so thrilling that after seeing the movie, Kim wanted to cut her waist-length hair. She clipped a photo of the violet-eyed actress out of *Ciné Monde*. Over Duc's favorite meal of clay pot catfish and seafood sweet and sour soup, she slid the picture beside his bowl. He eyed it flatly and continued slurping.

Finally, he said, "Uh-huh, the girl from that *Tin House* movie."

"*Cat on a Hot Tin Roof*, silly. But how about her hair? I want to get mine cut like that." Kim rolled up her folds of blue-black hair and held it at the nape of her neck.

"I love you the way I married you," he said. He took her hands and flattened his palms against hers, causing her hair to unroll down her back.

"But Duc . . ." she pulled her hair up again and smiled.

"No," he said and excused himself from the table, fish unfinished.

Kim cleared the table, washed the dishes, broke a bowl.

The following week, she was shopping on Sàigòn's fashionable Boulevard Bonard, when she found herself in front of the beauty salon. She stood at the window watching the scissors swim and glide through a lady's hair. A man waved her in and said, "Don't just stand there." Once in the salon seat, the hairdresser gathered her hair as she had done for Duc and nudged her chin toward the mirror. He said, "*Quelle jolie*," and whispered in her ear, "This cut will accentuate your already elongated neck. You'll be a swan among mortals."

Kim said, "But my husband will hate it."

He said, "Then your husband's a fool, darling."

She sat vigilant, watching her tresses falling to the floor.

With each snip, she felt the stiffness in her shoulders loosening, the burden of heavy hair no longer straining her neck. She had worn it long since her school days. She could still feel the thick thumping of the braid against her back, skipping rope. She remembered how it would get in her way, scratch her eyes, cause her to trip up. She hated how the boys yanked at it. Later, she used the long layers as a shield, hid behind it when the boys grew into men and stared. On the red leather chair, Kim slowly began to admire the new cut. She liked the way it revealed the shape of her skull, its ability to capture her expressions with clarity, and most of all, how it forced her to be brave.

That evening, Kim felt shaky preparing dinner. She had the maid clean the house over and over. She put on Duc's favorite traditional dress. When the brass doorknob rattled, she reached for the back of her bared neck. She greeted Duc at the door. He wore his ARVN officer's uniform. She leaned in to hug him. He took a step back, hands to his side, and stared at her. She lunged to kiss him, but he turned, giving her only his strained jaw to look at. Under his breath he said, "You look like a whore," and then tramped inside tracking red dirt on her polished floors.

"What's wrong with you?" she screamed after him. "I've asked you to take your boots off in the house."

From the bedroom he screamed back, "I guess neither of us listens." He didn't speak to her for two weeks. And for two weeks Kim forbade the maid from scrubbing those muddy footprints.

Inside the theater, Kim reached between her feet for the M&Ms inside her purse. She squeezed Sophia's knee once she found the candy and held them out to her daughter. Sophia didn't respond. Kim whispered, "Chocolate." Sophia's eyes stared straight ahead. Kim tapped her daughter's hand. The little hands resisted, clutching the armrests.

Puzzled, Kim turned to the screen and in larger than life techno-color got her response. Ample breasts and bare butts jiggled in her face. The nurses were completely nude, slithering about on the floor. They had wild manes and smoky eyes. Their rhinestone collars glittered around their necks like leashes. They were crawling around, licking each other, cat-like. Kim slapped her hands over her daughter's eyes. The candy flew.

"Stop it, I can't see. Let go." Sophia tried to pry her mother's hands loose. The camera panned up. Before her, the man stood naked, his penis fully erect. Kim gasped.

When they began to do what they did Kim was unable to look away, unable to move. When they began making noises, she was shaken from her paralysis. She didn't have enough hands to cover the child's ears too. She gathered their jackets and rushed her daughter out. Sophia cried, digging her heels into the bald carpet of the cinema floor. A bearded man in an aisle seat cringed at them. Outside, beneath sunlight, the girl's neck was still craned toward the movie screen, fighting each step home. She didn't want to leave her first ever outing to a movie. As they crossed the street, Kim heard a cat-call followed by a slow steady whistle. She thanked God, Buddha, and every Bodhisattva she could recall, that Bao hadn't come too.

Back at the 22nd Avenue house, she realized that Bao wasn't at his place because he was at hers. Kim stood in the middle of the living room and told her family, "I'll never understand this country. I thought we came because it would make more sense here." The women were watching TV on one end of the room and the men were drinking beer and roasting cuttlefish on the other.

Her son sat with his uncles. He was fidgeting with the mobile phone on the table and didn't even look at her. She said, "Careful you don't burn yourself, love." Marcel's eyes didn't lift. He was probably mad she hadn't taken him along to the movies. Kim had insisted he go to the park with his uncles. She wanted him to run around and kick a ball. She wanted him to do *boy things*, all the things she couldn't provide because his father was locked away in a prison in central Vietnam.

The men laughed so hard tears streamed down their reddened cheeks when she described *The Pussycats*. She realized then that they were already drunk. She played into it, told them about the naked women crawling around but left out the part about the man. This morsel she would save for the women, in the kitchen, over food. But first, she needed to stew it over so she could interpret her own gasp of disbelief and unwanted arousal. She hadn't seen a man or more accurately a *man's* in years.

Her older sister Huong asked, "How are we supposed to raise our children in a place like this?"

Her sister-in-law Trang asked, "How was a child permitted into this kind of establishment in the first place?"

The women sat in a row, crossed their arms, shook their heads and tssked their disapproval. From the other side of the room, her youngest brother Tri, who had lived in America the longest of them all said, "Don't blame the business owner. It's America, capitalism."

Bao waved a slice of cuttlefish in his hand and said, "You get what you pay for, remember?" As if it were a stage, he joined her in the middle of the living room floor and said, "Pussycat in English is the same as Butterfly in Vietnamese." He tossed the dried fish in his mouth. "She knew that!" He chomped on his food and bared his teeth to her. All her brothers laughed.

Kim said, "We have the same lesson plan at school and yet *somehow* he's an expert on these matters." At this, the rest of the women roared too.

The only person who didn't laugh was her oldest brother Lam who sat placid and sipped at his beer. He was the patriarch of the family and Bao was his best friend. Lam stated, "Little sister, Bao's only offering advice of one who's like an older brother to you."

Lam's wife said, "Ah, it just goes to show the Americans are much smarter than the Viet Cong, see? Here, the evil is masked cunningly." Trang doubled over on the brown corduroy couch laughing at her own joke. She had to cross her arms to hold her breasts down. As a teen she had been all curves and hazel eyes. It landed her on billboards for Coca-Cola and they paid her with a lifetime's supply. Lam explained his wife's weight saying it was all the soda she drank during her modeling days. Nobody dared mention her fat French father and genetics playing a part.

Later when they were alone in the kitchen, Trang squeezed Kim's hands in the pillows of her own and whispered, "I'm afraid my husband fears nothing, just kittens and butterflies leading to . . . birds and bees."

In this house there were always secrets and alliances. There were the things everyone was supposed to know. For example, that Huong was an insomniac, so if she was sleeping, it meant tipped- toes for the entire house. And then there were the things one knew but pretended not to know, like big Trang's mixed blood, or Lam's volatile temper, or the fact that Huong and her husband no longer had sex. So if Viet is sleeping out in the hallway, don't ask. But be careful you don't trip over his body in the middle of the night on your way to the bathroom. This was what it meant to live with your extended family, an entire nuclear family to a room, in a three-bedroom house.

That night little Sophia fell asleep immediately, exhausted from her fits of crying. Marcel stayed quiet, withholding his affection, stubborn like his father. Kim changed as usual behind a sheet dotted with faded blue cornflowers, hung in the corner of the room. "If you're nice, I'll read you Father's letter," she said. She raised her arms, quickly pulling her pajama top over her head. Kim couldn't stop thinking about the women on the big screen. She longed for their abandon, the way they had stretched and curled with nothing on except for those rhinestone collars with the little heart shaped name-tags dangling from their necks like jewels.

Kim asked Marcel to scoot his younger sister to the far side of their bed. She reached into the bedside drawer and pulled out the familiar grainy envelope, marked *par avion*. She received Duc's letters with pure relief. These thin sheets and tight scrawls were the only proof that her husband was still alive.

Duc's first words, *I love you. I miss you. Prison teaches you this, to not waste time. The best comes first, don't save anything for last.* Kim whispered her husband's words into her son's ear. Marcel closed his eyes and pulled the blanket to his chin. His father said, *get good grades, listen to your mother, take care of your sister.* She told him that his father was proud of him. She left out the lines from a husband to a wife that said *I miss your smooth skin and your soft touch . . . . I do not think I will ever be released from the fate of this grave site . . . . I want my son to grow up with a father. You must move on. Remarry . . . . You have always been and will always be the great love of my life.*

She covered her face with the letter, trying to gather Duc's scent. She had read it at least ten times since its arrival. But the last line destroyed her each time. *You have always been and will always be . . . .* It wasn't the voice of the hot-tempered, hard-headed man she knew. Only a defeated man would give up his woman. She felt her eyes welling up and quickly wiped it away.

Marcel asked, "Are you sad, Mama?"

She put her pointing finger over her lips and then tip-toed

down the hallway. She feared waking her brother and sister-in-law and their three sons until she remembered that the boys were spending the night with their "cool uncle Tri" and felt a pang of guilt for not having encouraged Marcel to go along too. Here she was reading him love letters, crying, and turning him into a mama's boy instead.

At the end of the corridor, Kim saw the couple's door slightly ajar. She reached to shut it, unprepared for the silhouette of Trang's torso against the starkness of the full moon. Trang straddled Lam, allowing him to support her tremendous mass. The bun her sister-in-law wore by day now cascaded free and flowing down her back. Kim didn't want to watch, but her feet were anchored, and the motion was intoxicating. They thrashed and swayed, and it appeared to her like a visual symphony. The momentum increased until it became an urgent rhythmic staccato and then the headboard pounded into the wall, a final crescendo. She heard Lam saying, "Quiet," trying to restrain his wife's reckless cries.

In the bathroom, Kim broke down and cried, resenting what she had witnessed, this flaunting of what fate and destiny had taken from her. She reread Duc's letter again. *I miss your smooth skin and soft touch.* A man always missed the warmth and softness of a woman. She yearned for the opposite, for his firmness, the rigid angles, the span of his back that stretched like endless steppes and the emerald fields of home.

Kim had been a virgin on her wedding night. As the baby girl of the family, she received a lot of frantically whispered advice. Lan, her oldest sister, (the one who insisted in staying in Vietnam) had told her to lie still. If she wiggled too much, her husband might not believe she was a virgin. Huong, her middle sister, the aspiring actress, told her to wiggle a little, and sigh, sounds were sexy. They went on about things being too big or too tight, or small and dry, not to mention the pain. When her new husband climbed on top of her, Kim was confused, unclear if she should lay stiff as a board or pounce around. Before he had even entered her, she began making noises. After nine long months of anticipation, Duc flopped on his back and said to the ceiling, "Please tell me this is a joke, God." Kim confessed, revealing her sisters' secrets. Together they laughed, picturing Lan lying like a sack of potatoes and Huong wiggling around like a fish. Kim didn't mind not consummating her marriage on her wedding night because her young husband caressed her, kissed her in places that had never known the lushness of a kiss, gave her new secrets all for herself.

For their honeymoon, they picked the Da Lat countryside for its scenic waterfalls and oceans of wildflowers. On the first day, caught in a shower, they ran for cover and happened onto a hidden grove of trees, a black-green canopy of pines. Kim was drenched, and Duc said, matter-of-factly, looking at her in her traditional white tunic, "I love your dark nipples." Against the trunk of a grand old pine, standing up, her husband made love to her for the first time. She held her palms flat against the cracked bark. Big great drops splattered on top of her head, the leaves clapped the applause of an audience a stadium away, and the winds howled feverish approval. Kim felt more alive than she'd ever felt and yet vulnerable, animal-like. Their lovemaking was as natural as breathing or sleeping. It imitated hunger. She promised herself, on the spot, that she would never belong to anyone else.

As Kim rocked in place on the toilet seat, she had to stuff away her thoughts of Bao. Looking around the bathroom, she noticed the mildewed tiles and the crooked floor, the splintered wood and the loose doors, she saw how slippery everything had become in her life. With this realization, she forgave her brother and sister-in-law. In this crowded old house, a slammed drawer or a loud laugh, a soft breeze, or a bit of gossip, just about anything could crack open, revealing even the slightest of indiscretions.

Mornings had to be tightly orchestrated on 22nd Ave. There were twelve people and only one bathroom between them all. Kim told the children "Brush your teeth so your teachers know you're not the children of peasants." She said, "Skip the shower but at least wet your hair down so you don't look like a refugee." She dried their hair but had no time to dry her own.

Kim arrived to her English as a Second Language class looking like a wet stray. Bao saved a desk for her and lifted the books beside him. When she sat down, he clawed at his desktop and smirked. It reminded her even more of his reputation as a tomcat before he married. In Sàigòn, he'd strut around the city with a camera dangling from his neck. Once when she was a teenager, she let Bao watch her reading beneath a lemon blossom in their courtyard. It was fragrant springtime, and the pollen made her brave. She lay on her side propped up on an elbow and smiled at him every couple of pages. He approached, asking her to pose. She allowed him one quick snap before she ran away because she was young, scared, and swollen by the thought of him even then.

A decade later, he was the only man in her life who wasn't family.

They'd gotten into the habit of going for coffee at the Dunkin' Donuts after class. Outside, it began to rain. Bao lit his cigarette and smoked it with relish. Over steaming cups he said, "Careful you don't get sick, going outside when your hair is still wet."

Kim shook her head, allowing the damp ends to splay out against her face. She said, "I'll use the blow dryer when I get to beauty school," when he reached across the table with fingertips stained from nicotine and without a hint of self-consciousness, brushed the hair from her cheek.

They sat nestled inside their booth watching the passersbys outside in trench coats and newspaper hats. Kim said, "I can't believe Sophia and I walked to the movies just yesterday." She blushed immediately regretting the mention of those *Pussycats* again.

"My sons would play in the rain naked and roll around in the mud. It made my wife crazy," he said.

"It would have made me crazy, too. I hate mud in the house," she said thinking back to Duc and his muddy footprints.

 She watched Bao put out his cigarette and tuck the remaining stub back in its box. "I miss home," he said. "American rain is ugly, gray, too much like that war."

"Have you heard yet?" she asked. "Have you gotten any news?"

He wrestled with his hands and then slid the cigarette box across the table with a flicker of disgust. He looked out at the rain and said, "I should have waited for them."

Kim placed both palms against the table's edge and stopped the box as if she were a goalie. "You had no choice," she said.

"No," he said, "I could have stayed, but I chose to leave."

"They were locking up American sympathizers. Who would you help locked up? Would you help your wife the way Duc is helping me?" Her hands trembled with her jolt of fury. Her voice was full of strain. Everyone knew that once he turned his camera from snapping pretty girls to documenting the decimated villages and then the war crimes, Bao's life was at risk. She wanted to tell him that he was being stupid, irrational. But her reflection in the window revealed to her the disgraceful transparency of a schoolgirl. Instead, she shut up. She slid out a cigarette and lit up.

They said nothing, sitting in silence for what seemed like a long while, until Bao finally spoke. "What happened with Sophia yesterday, at least you got that. It made me realize that my boys will probably be men by the time I see them. I have to become a citizen before I can be a sponsor. Did you know that? Who knows how long that'll take?" After six months, alone in a new country, Bao told Kim that he finally understood the depths of loneliness, its tendency to weaken the mind. "That's why widows and prisoners are permanently changed," he said.

Kim stroked the backside of his hand only once. She wondered which was worse. To be stuck in Vietnam while you knew your husband was free? Or to be free while your husband was imprisoned?

After an entire afternoon of beauty school and inhaling nail polish remover at Miss Marty's Hair Academy and Esthetic Institute, Kim returned home to the smells of sautéed onions and fried fish. Inside the cluttered kitchen Trang stood over a cutting board with her head bent low. Without looking up she lifted her knife and pointed toward the window. "Playing," she said. "It's a good day. No fights and no crying." She leaned in with her great weight and halved an onion. "Tri's bringing the boys back and he'll be bringing some friends over too. He wants to introduce us to Monday Night Football. 'An American tradition,' he said. 'Just potato chips,' he said. But my husband said it's dishonorable to have people over with no food to offer."

Kim rolled up her sleeves. When Huong came home she joined in too. When her youngest brother Tri arrived with his friends, they *wowed* at all the food. "Four variations of fish sauces to choose from alone?" The single men said they hadn't seen anything like it since they left their moms and sisters back in Vietnam.

Tri pulled Kim aside and said, "I told you guys just chips and dip."

"I don't even know what dip is," she said.

"Sauce from a can," he sighed.

Often it seemed that her own brother was an alien to her. Although there was only a three-year age difference between them, it was clear that his years in America had changed him. As the baby boy of the family, Tri was sent to America to get a Western education so that he could return with an American degree and be a sure bet for Vietnamese Parliament. Her parents would have never guessed when they sent him away that the American War would end with a Communist victory, that they would never see their youngest son again. However, it was Tri's U.S. residency that allowed him to sponsor them from the refugee camp. Otherwise, they likely would have ended up in Australia, or Germany, or France, since America was top on everyone's wish list.

Tri asked, "Who else is coming with all this?" He reached for his wallet. "You guys can't afford this."

She said, "It's okay, you've given us enough," and pushed his money away.

Kim dragged him to the ancestral shrine where framed portraits of their deceased parents sat beside a platter of fruit and some burning incense. "Look," she said, "I prayed for your team to win."

Tri said, "It's kind of you Sis, but you should save your prayers for the big games. This isn't the Super Bowl. It's not even the Play-Offs." He flapped at the collar of his red number sixteen jersey. "It's hot. I need a beer."

Just as the game began, Bao and Lam arrived. From the kitchen, Kim watched him shaking hands and greeting her siblings. As soon as he turned, she shrank behind the swinging door and stayed in the kitchen with the women and kids. Sophia hung on Kim's thigh meowing for food. Kim shushed her and said, "Stop that. You'll starve in this world if you don't speak properly."

The men in the living room were getting rowdier with each beer. When Kim peeked out, Bao caught her and waved her out.

The men progressed from beer to cognac. The women slowly inched into the circle. They passed the few remaining beer cans around. They made an excuse of it, saying, "We don't want to waste anything."

The 49ers were ahead. The men jumped out of their seats cheering. On the screen, a man on the red team caught a ball thrown from a great distance. He leapt straight up into the air and with the very tips of his fingers barely grasped the edge of the ball until he cradled it in his arms and protected it against his belly. Afterward, he flung it into the ground. The other team members hugged him and some were so happy they even patted his bottom. He was a big bear of a man and everyone agreed he was the best athlete on the team.

But Tri said, "Dwight Clark? No way, the best is right here baby," pointing to the name Montana stretched across his back and then doing a stomp and clap before shaking his butt. All the kids giggled.

Bao said, "Try some," and handed his cognac to Kim. She acquiesced when the women egged her on. She liked how relaxed she felt after only two sips. Lam was rip-roaring drunk and didn't object. He was busy strumming his guitar and singing pop songs from the old country for the kids. Marcel sat on the floor, resting his hands in his lap, mesmerized. Sophia pulled at her brother's shirttail, needy for his attention. When this didn't work, she meowed in his ear.

Bao turned to Kim and asked, "Is there food left?"

They went to the kitchen and Kim offered to make him a plate. She gave him a scoop of rice topped with chicken curry, pan-fried noodles, shrimp salad, and spring rolls. She wanted to give him everything, all the good stuff.

Bao gestured to the freshly sliced peppers placed at the corner beside the basil. "That's something my wife did." He was looking at her as if he wanted to say something more, when Kim was certain there was nothing more, that there could not be.

"Duc liked spicy food, too," she said. She felt the alcohol simmering inside and feared she had had too much.

"Any word on his release?"

Kim ran cold water from the faucet and distracted herself by preparing tea. She found the kettle almost too heavy to bear. She had become a weaker woman than she used to be. She stood on her toes reaching for the cups in the cupboards overhead. Bao grabbed them for her and stood behind her so close the tips of his shoes tapped her heels. Her hands shook when he handed her the delicate cups. She thanked him without meeting his eyes.

The kids were running down the hall. She heard their little footsteps echoing on the old floorboards. Marcel shouted, "Stop it or I'll tell!" Kim froze, momentarily believing her seven-year-old son could see through walls, had seen through her.

When she lifted her face to Bao's she hoped it was composed, expressionless, withholding. She suspected she had failed because her lips were trembling. He sat next to her, closer than usual inside the arm of the breakfast nook. They were lit beneath a naked dangling bulb. Kim cracked open the window and rested her head against the windowpane. Her nieces Elle and Michelle were outside gossiping. Frenzied chatter rushed in with the fog. One of them uttered an American boy's name, something like Tyler or Kyle and then both girls fell into a gaggle of a giggling fit.

Bao blew out a defeated half-chuckle and said, "Me and you, we're the same. We're almost living, but not quite."

"We're living. My children don't want for anything."

"I'm talking me and you." He squeezed her hand beneath the table. "I wish things were different," he said. She settled her gaze into Bao's red-veined eyes and wondered if he too slept with a pillow cradled between his legs, lost sleep because he cried at midnight, woke up before dawn grabbing for a warm body that wasn't there.

Kim was scared but continued holding Bao's hand. He interlaced his fingers between hers, pushing deep so that the dips and grooves of bone and flesh became a solid fist. With his other hand, he reached over and touched the nape of her neck with cautious fingertips. He swallowed hard and she watched his Adam's apple rise and fall. "I like your hair short. Brings out your face," he said. "I'm glad to see it's not wet anymore." He inched in with cognac and cigarettes on his breath.

Kim let him kiss her shoulder, while she watched the door. She let his lips graze her neck, while she studied for shadows under the slit of it. She let him place his hand on her thigh as she listened for approaching footsteps. She thought she could smell her own fear. She thought her heart would burst. And yet she couldn't help but smell his scent, couldn't help imagining how his mouth would feel opening upon her. Her husband had said move on, but would he forgive her? Or would she live with a lifetime of footprints stamped on her back?

Kim understood desire in its true form as a thirst, as a yearning so deep, it meant risking tragic consequences for the promise of only one sip.

Bao asked, "Can we go somewhere?"

But where? She pictured her and Bao in the cluttered hall

way closet the kids called the phone booth, panting and grasping between the interview clothes, reaching for an arm to discover a broom handle, squirming between winter jackets and cardboard boxes. From this nook in the kitchen, in the central room of a shared house, Kim heard her sisters in the living room asking the men if they were finished with their food. She heard her brothers grumble and sigh. There was the clatter and ding of plates being stacked one on top of the other.

Bao said, "Please, anywhere," and this time it was his lips that trembled. He squeezed her hand even harder, not letting go, leaning in closer, waiting for her reply. She could feel his warmth radiant on the tips of her lashes.

The kettle began to cry but they ignored it. Kim wanted to give herself over. She wanted to be like *The Pussycats*, arched back and easy abandonment. She wet her lips and waited. Bao's mouth had barely skimmed hers when the boom of her oldest brother's voice jolted her backward. From the other room, Lam shouted something incomprehensible, although she guessed it to be the punch line of a joke when a huge wave of laughter spilled into the kitchen. The tide of laughter peaked and crested, crashing to the shattering of breaking glass, followed by her daughter's wail, screeching louder than the crying kettle. These decibels of life coalesced layer by layer, until the pressure of so much wanting under one roof finally swept the kitchen door wide open.

Sophia ran through and hopped into her mother's lap. She cried about the glass she'd accidentally dropped and broken. Kim comforted her by smoothing down her hair. As was Sophia's new habit, she meowed to show her gratitude. But this time, Kim didn't scold her. She continued petting the sleek black hair. Beneath her hand, her daughter purred.

EVERYTHING FORBIDDEN

The healthy take care of the sick. A youth respects his elders. Older siblings take care of younger siblings.. It had rained recently and Golden Gate Park smelled of tamped-on eucalyptus leaves stewing atop damp soil. The pungent acidity of it sliced through her. It put a spring in her step. Her chanting matched her pace while her eyes scanned the park grounds. Huong needed the perfect stick to c o gió her oldest daughter with. She needed to treat the girl before Elle's condition worsened.

Beside Huong, her nine-year-old was on her hands and knees digging through a mountain of leaves. Michelle was small for her age and in her puffy brown coat with the white stitching looked like a little burrowing squirrel. Huong wondered if Michelle's size was caused by their internment at the refugee camp. Maybe being surrounded by so much illness and death during her formative years had stunted the girl's growth. In fact, she shouldn't have been out at all on a day like today. Huong's guilt caused her to snap at the girl. "Pull your zipper up. Cover your throat. God knows I can't afford another sick child."

Michelle held out a branch. "This one?"

"No, too big, it should be small enough to fit inside here." Huong pointed to the hole in the middle of the Vietnamese coin. "About the size of your button," she said and caressed the white plastic sphere on Michelle's coat pocket.

Michelle offered another stick.

"That's too small," Huong said. "It has to be firm enough to pull wind from a sick person's chest."

It was December in San Francisco and winter had recently arrived. The wind was blustery and unyielding, raining down a storm of copper leaves over their heads. Huong's hair blew into her mouth. The foreign taste lay on her tongue like bitter shards of tin.

After four years in this country, Huong still wasn't accustomed to the cold. Summers in the city were bearable and even temperate once the sun chased out the fog. Unfortunately, those few golden months were over in a blink before winter came charging in, bone-chilling in a way that could crush you like a train. She blamed Elle's sickness on the dramatic climate change.

Since their arrival, Huong and Viet had been doing their best to get on and get by. They started off with no savings, no English, and only the clothes on their backs. Now, they had stable jobs. Huong joined the movement to make "computers the wave of the future" and worked as an electronics technician assembling circuit boards. Viet was a mailman. His pay wasn't great but the benefits were good since it was a government job. After four years of scratching by, they had saved enough to move out from the cramped 22nd Ave. house they had shared with her brother and sister and their kids.

Their landlord, the Japanese Baptist Church has said, "Choose God or get out."

Huong told Viet, "I want to become an American citizen. I believe in democracy. And I choose to be Buddhist." She was choosing freedom over the collective family unit. That was the moment of truth when she realized how slowly but surely

Americanized they'd become.

Her sister Kim had moved across the city to the Mission with her little Sophia and Marcel. Huong didn't worry about Kim. She was tough as nails, blade sharp, whip-smart and as soon as Duc was sponsored over, they'd be fine. Her brother Lam had followed his job with a computer software company to San Jose. He bragged that this place called Silicon Valley was the "Hollywood of the next decade." It was the new dream making machine in America. Despite his bravado, Huong hoped it was true for his sake and the sake of the boys.

Huong prayed this new job and the better pay would appease Lam's demons. Throughout the years on 22nd Ave., her insomnia made her witness to his tantrums. In the middle of the night, she could hear the slap of his belt on skin. The double insulated walls did nothing to muffle Trang's cries or the boys' pleading. Huong hated those thin walls. She hated what she had learned about her own brother; how his bitterness about this new life beset those he loved most. She hated the excuses she made for him in the mornings in order to look him in the eye again. And most of all, she hated that everyone in the house probably heard it too. Yet nobody spoke out in the cowardly name of not betraying one's blood. Not ever her, the self-righteous outspoken girl of the family. She hated what she had discovered about herself.

At their new apartment, Huong most cherished the new-found privacy in which to live her life. She didn't care that it wasn't beautiful. She didn't mind that it was a box-like duplex on the second floor, stuffed between people above and below like a sandwich. It was clean, in walking distance to the Park, and most importantly, it was all hers.

She could hear her father saying, "It has to have the right essence and the proper proportions to be a healing tool." He was known to be the best doctor in the South because he combined his French education with the folk methods. She prayed she had inherited his sensibility as she was sifting through a pile of twigs.

Michelle ran up bright-eyed and rosy-cheeked and said, "This is it." The little one was right. The stick fit right through the *xu*.

Huong said, "Let's keep looking."

Michelle said, "But why?"

"I'd like something smoother."

"Mom, it's impossible to find a smooth one."

Huong said, "Are you talking back to me? Do you know I have to use it as a handle? You want me to get calluses? My hand to bleed?"

Michelle rubbed her tennis shoes together. She scrunched up her face like a cabbage. "But I want to go play." She pointed into the fenced playground. Her attention was focused on a child spinning on a merry-go-round.

"Your sister's sick in bed and you want to play?"

"I wish I was sick like Elle. Sicker even!" Michelle began to cry. Snot ran down her lip. She sniffled, "You only love me when I'm sick."

The wind hurled more leaves at them and along with it the screeching laughter of children. The gurgling sounds of joy made Michelle cry even harder. Huong had no choice but to say, "Fine, for a few minutes, but go get cleaned up first."

She dropped Michelle's stick into her pink grocery bag. It went in with all the leaves they'd been gathering since sunrise: the grapefruit leaves from a neighbor's yard, the lime leaves by the pizza parlor, the lemon leaves beside the liquor store, and the eucalyptus leaves from the grounds of the park itself.

Huong settled on a wooden bench on the edge of the playgroud. She sat facing the slide. In front of her, a little boy rode down the aluminum slide. He reminded Huong of her son. He smiled at her when he scooted his butt off the shiny ramp. His dimples were big and fat and perfectly kissable. He was around the age her son would have been if he'd lived.

With only two kids, she didn't know how she had raised such a strangely selfish child, no consideration, and an ingrate to boot. When she was Michelle's age, there were so many kids in her family, they were called by numbers. "Girl number Five, go help Six and Seven bathe before dinner." In South Vietnam, odd numbers were deemed unlucky so the first-born was always designated number two.

Huong was girl number Four in a family of six children. Her boy would have been number Four just like her. If he was still alive she would call him her pinky, a term of endearment for the baby in the family. Every night before putting herself to bed, she wished for his return. Instead she was left with the memory of her baby boy, his still face stark white wrapped in a white sheet, right before she threw him overboard.

Huong wrapped her arms around her shoulders and rocked in place. *The healthy take care of the sick. A youth respects his elders. Older siblings take care of younger siblings.* She consoled herself by repeating the chant but this time she added a fourth tenant. *A parent passes before a child.*

Huong freed her arms to wave to the boy. He waved back and then ran inside the climbing dome. When he poked his head out, she waved again. "Hello," she said and smiled.

He stood before her and scratched his neck. Up close, he was much lighter-skinned than her boy. Her son had been the color of burnt caramel. Her sisters blamed it on the iced coffee she'd craved during her pregnancy. They said, "Thank god it's a boy because a girl that color would have been cursed." They called him *bé trai café au lait*. Four and Six thought the nickname was exceedingly smart. They even fought over who had coined it. Huong paid their bickering no mind. She was too busy loving his delicious smile and that candied skin.

The little boy who stood before her seemed like a sweet child. She didn't know what to say to him and thought she could give him a gift. She reached for a lemon she'd picked but felt it inappropriate to give sour fruit to a child. Finally, she decided to give him her Vietnamese coin. The *xu* glinted in her palm.

The boy snatched it up and smirked. "You liking the money huh? You are a smart boy." She tapped her temple and reached out to pet his glistening black hair. Her finger rested on the part at the center of his head. She held it there until she could feel warmth come through, and, with it, a strange sense of relief. It made her smile, causing her winter lips to rip. When she dabbed it, she saw blood on her fingertip. The boy's eyes widened as if frightened. He examined her finger and then stepped back. He dropped his coin.

Huong said, "Take, take, you're a smart boy, *no* problem." She emphasized the *o* the way the Americans did on TV to accentuate the sounds of ease, a worry-free existence.

He eyed the coin on the ground.

"*No* problem," she said again. He bent over and was about to reach for it when a pregnant woman arrived. She stepped out of the play box dragging sawdust with her. The debris landed on Huong's shoe although she ignored it and smiled to show that she was friendly. She sat still with her hands buried between her knees. She angled her face just slightly toward the sky. Huong had been beautiful all of her life and was used to people looking at her and then approving.

The woman's expression didn't soften. She pulled the boy's head into her belly and said, "I don't know if you read but there's a sign." She surveyed the area as if to determine Huong's relation to the children at play. There were a handful of white children, one mixed-race child, and a Hispanic child but no Asian kids. "Over there," she pointed, "there's a sign that says, 'No adults allowed unaccompanied by a child.'"

Huong tried to say that her daughter was in the bathroom. She was still formulating the sentence in English in her head when the woman whipped around and carried the boy to the other side of the playground.

At her foot, partly covered in sawdust, the coin winked. She couldn't tell if it was mocking or nice. She remembered the Vietnamese Prime Minister once saying to her, "Your face should grace our country's five-hundred-dollar bill." His eyes were fixed below her neck when he'd said it.

She was in her mid-twenties, still childless though newly married, and because her father was the Prime Minister's private doctor, the family had been invited to dine with the politician and his wife.

Huong said, "I'd rather be on a coin."

"But why?" he said, finally looking her in the eye. "Your image would be so much larger and clearer on a bill. Don't deprive the people. No, not a mere coin."

"But I'd prefer it. That way I could be loved by all the people of Vietnam, not just the rich, but loved by all."

The Prime Minister laughed and brushed her hand with his fingers before reaching for his empty drink. "Clever," he said with his pointing finger only inches from her nose. "You've got a clever one," he declared across the table and held his glass up as a salute to her father. Her husband, the young professor eyed them with pained curiosity. Her father from across the table put four fingers in the air to show his patient that he was keeping count. The Prime Minister ignored his doctor's orders. He signaled for another drink. He'd always been a reckless man.

Huong wasn't surprised then, when many years after that dinner party he was overthrown. Once American involvement was withdrawn, the country's economy faltered. A five-hundred-dollar bill eventually became worthless, used as toilet paper by some. Huong thought, not even a fool would use a coin to wipe his ass.

Huong was pocketing the coin when Michelle returned from the bathroom. "Come on," she said, "let's go."

"I thought you said I could play."

"I've changed my mind."

"But why?"

Huong didn't respond. On the way out, she saw the sign with its official red lettering that said, *No adults allowed unaccompanied by a child.*

Michelle kept tugging at her and asking, Why? Why? Why?

Huong said, "Do you want what happened to your brother to happen to your sister? Just so you can play?"

Michelle didn't utter another peep.

Back at home, Huong ran up the stairs and rushed into the apartment without a word to Viet. She checked Elle's temperature, making sure her husband had enough sense to keep a cool cloth on the girl's forehead.

"She slept mostly," said Viet, who'd been sitting at the girl's bedside. He put on his glasses and took the opportunity to get up and use the bathroom. "I think she'll be fine, some rest is what's needed."

Huong swept Elle's bangs off her forehead and felt her temperature. She opened her mouth to say something but Huong *shushed* her quiet saying, "Save your strength. Go back to sleep. I'll get everything ready for you," and tiptoed out the room.

In the kitchen, Huong angled the blinds to protect her herbs from the glare. She poured the leaves from the pink plastic bag inside a pot. She added baby ginger and slices of lemongrass too. The broth boiled until it steamed up the room. The smells of the room swept her back to the tropical humidity and orange groves of her youth.

Elle's legs buckled when she tried to get out of bed. She blamed it on her foot being asleep. But Huong didn't believe her. She panicked. She marched straight to the living room to find Viet. "Your daughter's close to dying and what do you do?"

He was absorbed in a game of chess with Michelle. "Did something happen? Is Elle okay?"

"What do you think happened? She can barely take a few steps to the kitchen."

"Stop exaggerating." He kept his voice low. "You scare everyone to death. It's bad luck, your being so pessimistic all the time."

Huong amplified her words not caring who heard. "Everyone would be dead if it weren't for me. Nobody else around here cares enough to worry. My God, to think to play games at a time like this."

Huong made Viet carry the girl from her bed into the kitchen. They placed her over the boiling pot with a towel draped on her head. Elle complained it was too hot.

Huong held the girl's hair out of her face. "Lean on me," she said. "We have to steam out the toxins before we can extract the wind." She enticed Elle into standing longer by encanting the list of dishes she would make for her over the week's course.

When they returned to the bedroom, Huong noticed that the sheets had been changed. On the nightstand, the *xu,* the bottle of Tiger brand menthol oil, and the stick were meticulously laid out on a white towel. She picked up the stick and rolled it between her palms. All the knots had been carved out. Viet said, "See, I don't spend *all* my time playing games, Boss."

She asked, "Did you remember to sterilize the *xu* in alcohol?"

He said, "I wouldn't dare forget," and shut the door behind him.

Elle took off her nightgown and lay on her belly. Huong climbed on the mattress and straddled Elle's lower back. "Is this okay?" she asked. It was difficult to find a comfortable spot on the girl's narrow torso.

"Mom, I thought you said a lady always sits with her knees touching."

"It's true."

"Well, you're not."

"I only break rules for the health of my children," she said.

Outside, the city buses were loading and unloading passengers below. Huong dotted drops of the menthol oil on Elle's back. She scraped with the coin and followed her map of green markings like roadside reflectors in the night. Her strokes were gentle without being so soft that the effects of the medicine wouldn't absorb. She worked from the spine outward, careful to place the coin at an angle and only along the edge of each rib. The blood rose to the surface and pink dots streaked across the girl's skin. In the areas where Elle had stored the most wind, it immediately turned the purplish yellow shade of deep bruising.

Her daughter asked, "How much longer will this take? How much longer will I be sick? Do you think I'll be good enough to play in the soccer game Thursday?"

Huong focused on Elle's back, concentrating on the topography of the girl's illness, deciphering from rising bruises the recovery period. After the scraping, she massaged oil into the girl's throat, behind her ears, and above her chest. Huong finished the treatment by pounding her fists lightly up and down Elle's back to re-invigorate circulation. When she finished she commanded, "No soccer for at least a week."

Elle reached for her nightgown but Huong wouldn't let her put it on. "Were you going to put on that dirty rag you've been sweating in all night? There are probably a million germs having babies inside the fabric by now." She knew it was her daughter's favorite nightgown and put it aside to be personally hand washed.

For dinner Huong made chicken porridge because the wet rice would be easier going down a sore throat. She paired it with stir-fried *cai be xanh* because the greens had a medicinal cooling effect. Standing over the stove with her chopsticks in hand Huong wondered if she would ever again possess the finances or the inspiration to make the dishes she once secretly considered her art. She used to make her own *pâté*, a duck Montmorency no one in Sàigòn had ever tasted the likes of before, and in the summer months, a jackfruit ice cream from scratch. Her dinner parties used to be written up in *Tin Sáng's* society pages. How quickly life changes in a year or even a day. Right as Huong finished this thought ambulance sirens shrieked by and then slipped away quick as a ghost. It was a reminder of how the big turns in her life really happened: the click of a grenade, the snap of a suitcase, a child's last breath.

After dinner, Huong let Elle go directly to the television without helping with clean up. Michelle grumbled, again saying she wished she too were sick because she was responsible for all of the dishes. Huong held her ground, knowing Viet would inevitably come to the little one's side.

On Monday morning, Elle stayed home from school. Huong heard the girl coughing incessantly. She was grateful she worked the night shift precisely for these unforeseen events. This way, Huong was always available in the days and Viet covered the evenings and they didn't have the expense of a sitter. Having the day also allowed Huong the opportunity to make the dishes she believed would yield the speediest recovery. She disliked her daughters missing any school. Huong prayed for two things every night at their ancestral shrine: good health and good grades.

On Tuesday, the coughing lessened. Her temperature had dropped. But still, Huong said it would be safer to wait.

On Wednesday, Elle was ready for school. Huong woke up early to make egg noodle soup for breakfast. She looked on while her family slurped away, splattered on her tablecloth, and talked with their mouths full. She bit her tongue and didn't reprimand them once.

In the afternoon, she rushed to greet the girls at the bus stop before going to work. Usually, she met them only on special occasions like birthdays and holidays. Michelle was clearly excited to see her. Elle offered a weak smile from behind the grimy glass of the yellow school bus.

"Remind your father that the halibut soup needs to be boiled but then turned off immediately," she said. "And don't put too much fish sauce in the noodles because it overwhelms the grilled beef." To celebrate Elle's recovery, Huong made each girl her favorite dish.

Huong held Elle by the shoulders at arms distance to examine her. "How was school?"

"Fine."

"You don't look okay. Worse than this morning."

Elle looked down at the sidewalk. She wiggled out of reach.

"Are you tired?"

"Yeah, I just want to go home Mom."

Huong sat at the electronics assembly line preoccupied all night. She didn't like Elle's mood and couldn't understand it. When she spoke of it at break, her co-workers dismissed her fears. "You know how girls are at that age. All those hormones out of whack."

The next morning, Huong stayed in bed. She let the sounds floating outside her door drift by. She heard Viet and the girls shuffling around the kitchen, opening and closing cupboards, the tightening of thermos lids and clanging of lunch boxes as they packed their lunches. She kept her shutters drawn and the lights out. She stared at the ceiling. Had Elle not wanted vermicelli noodles yesterday? Was it no longer her favorite? Was she getting spoiled with the extra attention? For her daughter's own good, Huong decided the niceness was ending. Everyone was the same, even your own flesh and blood. As soon as you show some heart, they crush you.

Huong got out of bed after she heard the locking of deadbolts and then the footsteps running down the stairs, (something she always warned them not to do). She went to the kitchen, misted her basil, then her mint, and then put on some tea. Huong had just taken a seat when the doorbell rang. "Mrs. Le, may I speak with you please?" It was a woman's voice calling her name.

She froze, hoping the person would go away. She almost never had visitors.

Again she heard, "Mrs. Le, are you home?" The chiming doorbell was now accompanied by a determined knocking.

Through the crack of the door, Huong saw a woman of her height but with hair so big it made her appear many inches taller. "My name is Irene Pacheco. Are you Elle's mother?"

Huong nodded and unlatched the rusty chain.

The woman pulled a clipboard from her oversized purple

purse. She checked the number on the apartment door, and said, "You're the stepmother of Elle Thao Tran at A.P. Giannini Middle School, correct?"

Huong blinked at the term "stepmother." She said, "I am the mother of Elle."

Irene Pacheco said, "Sorry." She checked her clipboard. "The different last names must have thrown me off."

Huong said, "Women in my country don't change their names when they marry." She continued more urgently, "Is my daughter okay?"

"I'm from Child Protective Services Mrs. Le. That's what I'm here to talk to you about." Huong felt the back of her throat closing when she heard the word *child* and *protect*. "May I come in Mrs. Le? I just have a few questions. It won't be long."

Huong opened the door and the woman stepped inside. The woman walked down the hallway ahead of her. She slowed to peer inside the bedrooms and wrote notes on her legal pad the entire time. From behind, Huong said, "I can offer you tea."

"No thanks," said Irene Pachecho, without even turning around to make eye contact.

Huong was proud of her modest apartment and was discouraged that this stranger she had let into her home didn't offer a compliment or any niceties. Despite the ill-mannered behavior, Huong still felt obliged to have something to offer. Huong excused herself to the kitchen in order to rummage through the cupboards. She was relieved to find a tin of buttermilk cookies. The box clanked against the glass coffee table when she set the cookies down. It made a violent sound like cymbals crashing.

Irene Pacheco stood at the living room wall studying Viet's framed diplomas. She turned around and said, "This is nothing to be alarmed about Mrs. Le," and took a seat. "I only have a few routine questions." She turned the page of her yellow pad. Her nails were peach and nicely polished. "How many children do you have?" she asked.

Huong almost said, three, automatically counting her son. She corrected herself in time and in perfect English said, "I have two children."

"How old are your children?" she asked.

"My daughter Elle is twelve years old. My daughter Michelle is nine years old."

"And how long has your family been in this country?"

"Four years."

Huong's eyes kept returning to the untouched cookies. "Please I invite you," she said and opened her palm to encourage Irene Pachecho to partake.

Irene shook her head, smiled without showing teeth, and continued. "Is your family happy in America?"

Huong was used to people asking if she liked it here. And she always said yes because she imagined it was better than being stuck with the Viet Cong. But happiness, that was different. It was a personal question. On one hand, she thought the girls were happy. They seemed to like American culture. They only spoke to each other in English now. They barely spoke about any memories of the old country. They loved pizza, and roller-skating, pop music and sports, all things American.

But was she happy? She asked herself this every day. And Viet, was he happy? Did he prefer delivering mail to the lectures he used to give on Confucius and Kant? Huong sipped her tea and noticed Irene Pacheco tapping her pen against her clipboard. She finally decided to say, "Yes, we want to become American citizens." Then she added, "You must like a drink? Coke? Coffee? Water?"

Huong was grateful Irene Pacheco at least agreed to water although it was a bit unexpected because she'd heard that Americans loved soda. She then thought that perhaps Irene Pacheco was on a diet because she was overweight. Americans were supposedly always dieting too. Huong went to retrieve fruit from her ancestral shrine.

Irene Pacheco said, "Please, you don't need to go through the trouble. I had a late breakfast. I need your full attention." She pushed the plate of sliced mandarin wedges aside.

Irene Pacheco cleared her throat. She said the words of the proceeding question slower than she had the rest. "How do you discipline your children, Mrs. Le?" Huong leaned in trying to listen better. She squinted her eyes. Irene said, "Let me rephrase it. What do you do when your daughter, Elle, does something you don't like?"

Huong wondered if the woman was implying Elle was a bad girl. Huong said, "She a good girl. Good student. Helps me at home."

"Children aren't perfect, Mrs. Le. What do you do when she misbehaves? Disobeys you?"

"Ah, only sometimes. Like in the morning, I always say to them don't run down the stairs. It is too dangerous. You can fall down. And this morning, I hear them running too fast down the stairs." Huong crossed her arms and shook her head to show her displeasure.

"So you *yell* at them when they don't listen?"

Huong wondered if it was a trick question. She said, "I tell them don't run, everyday, don't run. But they are stubborn. One was born in the year of the cat and the other a mouse. She is tricky."

Irene Pacheco flipped through a few pages of notes and then continued. She hunched her shoulders forward as if she was going to confide a secret to a friend. She said, "Mrs. Le, I am here because Elle's teachers are concerned about her…"

"She acted bad in school?" Huong was ready with profuse apologies. Wait till Viet finds out. She held a dark desire to see his sunny, all-loving exterior crack. If Mr. Professor didn't reprimand the girl for this one, she would hoard this stone as proof against his indulgence for a lifetime.

But the woman said, "No, Mrs. Le. Elle's teachers are concerned because she has bruises up and down her back." For the first time during her visit, Irene Pacheco sat back against the couch.

Huong nodded. She wanted to show she understood so that Irene Pacheco would continue on with her point. Irene Pacheco picked up her water glass and drank. When she gulped down the entire glass and then set it down and didn't say anything more, Huong realized that the other woman was waiting for her to speak. They sat facing each other in silence. Finally, Irene Pacheco leaned forward and said, "Do you have anything to say Mrs. Le?"

Huong thought it was an odd thing to say after the question and answer pattern that had already been established. Huong thought about the bruises Irene Pacheco had brought up. The wind had gotten in deep this winter. The bruises were darker than they had ever been in past treatments. My poor Elle, she thought. Huong wanted to try and explain this when she heard the other woman take a deep breath. Irene Pacheco said, "Mrs. Le," and then she paused to take another deep breath. "Your daughter told her school counselor that *you* gave her the bruises."

Huong blinked. The way Irene Pacheco said "you" made her realize why this woman had come. She had sensed all along that the visit was out of the ordinary. But never would she have predicted the depths of her fall. A stranger had come into her home to accuse her of hurting her own child. In the most respected country in the world, such beast-like acts happened often enough that they actually had organizations to catch people at it. . And she, Huong Le who had come from one of Sàigòn's best families was targeted as somebody to be caught.

Huong wanted to cry but forbade herself. She would never show weakness before this hateful woman. But then her throat closed up and she couldn't stop coughing. Meanwhile, Irene Pacheco sat patiently and waited. She wanted Huong to say something. She handed Huong her now cold cup of tea.

When Huong said nothing, Irene Pacheco offered, "The other girls saw her back and told the teacher. Her P.E. teacher said she thought it strange that Elle was reluctant to participate. They were going to do soccer drills that day and that's Elle's favorite sport isn't it? She plays on the girls junior varsity team doesn't she?"

Huong remembered how she had discouraged Elle from joining. "The running around will build up your calves too big," she'd warned. "It's not pretty for a girl to have big legs," she'd advised. But Elle had laughed it off and now it was being used as some sort of deceitful evidence against her.

"Your daughter was ashamed. She didn't want to take off her shirt and have all the other girls see."

"What my daughter say?" After the timid peeps and squeaks and little smiles, her voice roared. Irene Pacheco's eyes widened. Huong glanced at Irene's manicured peach nails and saw before her a bully unaccustomed to anyone fighting back.

"Now calm down. Your daughter didn't implicate you. She said it was a…" Irene Pacheco flipped the pages of her legal pad and checked her notes. She located what she was searching for and ran her finger across the page. "She said it was 'a medical treatment.'"

"So why you come here? You say my daughter a lying? You

say I'm a lying?"

Huong was so angry she no longer cared about consequences. She raised herself from the couch, marched into her bedroom, and retrieved the silk bundle from her dresser drawer. *Let them lock me up,* she thought and dropped the items in Irene Pacheco's lap. Irene slowly opened up the silk folds. Her mouth maintained the shape of an O as she examined the little green bottle and the small, shiny, donut-like coin.

Huong scooped up the items as soon as Irene Pacheco set them back down. "This what I use for my daughter when she very sick." She shook the bottle and waved the coin in the air. She explained how she treated Elle. She told Irene Pacheco that her father had been the private doctor to diplomats, and politicians, the country's Prime Minister Nguyen Van Thieu! Irene Pacheco raised her brows. Her stiff hairdo lifted along with her expression. Huong grew so bold she put oil on herself and began scraping at her own neck to demonstrate. She swiveled her neck in small circles, sighing once, slightly audible, to illustrate the relief it gave. Irene Pacheco looked puzzled but she continued taking furious notes. Before she left, Irene Pacheco thanked Huong for her time. At the doorway, she even put her hand out as they said their good-byes.

Once she shut the door, Huong felt a rush of triumph. She told herself she'd beat down the devil today. Her hands were still shaking when she closed the windows and yanked the blinds over her beloved herbs. She retreated into her bedroom and used the last of her strength to throw the *xu* and the menthol oil away. She threw it with such force, the glass bottle shattered into pieces.

Huong locked the bedroom door, slammed the shutters shut, and crawled back into bed. She wrapped herself inside the covers and stayed sweating beneath them. She found solace in the wet heat. The room reeked of menthol. It burned her nostrils and made her eyes water and mixed with the tears streaming down her face.

She reflected back to the first time she was ever insulted. She was so fresh off the boat, she probably still smelled of the sea. Huong had gone to the Woolsworth with her daughters. When they reached the register, the cashier snapped gum in her face. It was intended to be a greeting. The cashier then said, "What's up?" She was just a girl, a teen, barely older than Elle's age now. And yet, when Huong didn't respond, the girl hissed to the other cashier, "They're so rude. I swear these Orientals don't know how to smile." Her daughters looked down at their feet. Their ears reddened.

Outside the store Elle asked her, "Did you hear what she said about you?"

Huong said, "No, what did she say?"

"How could you not hear her Mom?"

Huong said, "Where I come from, servants are seen not heard."

And then her eldest daughter told her, "*Mom*, we're not in Vietnam anymore."

Huong thought then, as she did now, everything forbidden, can't do anything, anywhere, anymore.

She was still in bed when her husband and daughters returned from school. Viet asked her, "Did something happen? Why aren't you at work? Why didn't you answer when I knocked? Thank goodness I had a key to the bedroom door. Are you okay, dear? Why does the room smell?"

As Huong knew he would, Viet explained the girl's side. "She tried to stay covered but the teacher made her change." "She didn't want to do P.E. because she was obeying your instructions." "She told them you'd never hurt her." "Won't you let her apologize to you?" Viet held Huong while she lay flat on her back, body slack, eyes closed, mute. She heard Elle crying in the other room. She wished she could hold her daughter. She wished she could console her. She loved her children desperately, but now understanding the burden of such a love, no longer wanted it.

When Viet left the room to comfort their daughter, Huong got out of bed to retrieve her *xu*. She dug in the wastebasket, numbed to the glass shards. Beneath the covers, red blooms stained her white sheets as she rolled the coin between her fingers as if a rosary. *Loved by all*, she had once said. Huong held strong to her conviction, to a time when she was right in every way.

QUIET AS THEY COME

Viet Tran raised his elbows, spread his wings, and was gliding through the white crane movement when he caught himself holding his breath. He tried his best to concentrate on a slow steady flow but was anxious and had to remember to exhale. He attempted his one-legged rooster posture, lost his balance, and had to brace himself on the couch's end. A wave of vertigo washed over him accompanied by a static buzzing in his ears. It imitated the roaring lull of the seas. It reminded him of how the dead always seemed to surface along with his dreams. Twenty years ago, Viet had seen himself as Chancellor at a University. Today, he would be content as an accountant, with a desk to sit at, a respectable salary.

Nobody would believe that Viet Tran had ever killed a man. His friends in Vietnam often described him as gentle, kind, a man of letters, fanatical about chess, a good family man. His co-workers from the post office would probably say he was a simple man, a hard worker, a great listener. Viet's physicality and bodily strength wouldn't be mentioned. And yet there was a time in history, between continents, when he had taken a man's life with his bare hands.

Slicing his palms through the air, Viet guided his chi into the golden platter, directing the energy clockwise and allowing the circle to grow with each rotation. His fingertips began to tingle and he'd just entered into a rhythm when he heard the flapping of sheets, the clacking of blinds, and then the patter of his wife's slippers on the plastic mats covering their floors.

The distraction ticked at him but he told himself, count your blessings. He reminded himself that just a year ago the *tai chi* was impossible when he, his wife, and their two daughters were all contained inside the four walls of one bedroom.

Huong said, "You should practice interviewing, not *tai chi*."

Viet said, "You can't practice for it."

"I can dye your hair," she said.

"You did it last month."

She combed her fingers though his hair. He lost his posture. "Why are you up so early?" he asked. She didn't hear him. Huong had moved on to the kitchen and was grinding her coffee beans.

His wife was a sensitive creature. She was a worrier and suffered from insomnia. The lack of sleep curled up in sulky half moons beneath her luminous eyes. Viet wanted to ask her for another thirty minutes for his practice, but he didn't. He didn't want her sullen, tucked away in her bedroom with the blinds drawn. Ever since the visit from Child Protective Services this past winter, Huong seemed to have grown even more tentative about the day-to-day activities of their lives. She had changed her work schedule at the electronics firm from nights to days. She claimed that in America, "The devil visits you not at night but in the daytime, when you're alone and vulnerable."

Huong remembered the CPS visit as an attack, an insult that she wore like a raw wound. Ever since the incident, without warning, an unforeseen slight could cause her to withdraw inside herself. Sometimes, Huong fortressed off from him and the girls for what could be days at a time.

Viet returned to his postures. He was determined to shut out the busy noise but heard rock music blaring from one room and a blow dryer firing from another. The girls were up now too. Huong tapped him with the TV remote. "Father, can you move over a little? I can't see."

In the waiting room at Linkenheimer LLP, Viet saw four other applicants. They were nicely dressed, attractive, well-groomed, and perhaps half his age. They reminded him of his students in the fall, at the start of the term, fresh-faced and eager, when school meant the promise of knowledge and smelled like a new book. Viet patted his hair, hoping to shift the gray into hiding. He shuffled the papers inside his manila folder. The person who had helped him put his resume together said, "You don't need to bring those diplomas from Vietnam." Nonetheless, Viet had taken them out from behind the glass frames in which they usually were displayed in his living room. He continued carrying these yellowed fading certificates to the interviews, reminders of who he was and what he'd once achieved.

The woman who gave him the written tests said, "Mr. Tran, you have a PhD in philosophy and a law degree too. Are you sure you're not overqualified?" Her expression was sincere and she asked it without the skepticism he sometimes heard.

"I be fortunate as state tax associate here, Miss."

She smiled and said, "Good luck, sir," and closed the door behind her. She left him with tax laws to manipulate, sales and use taxes, property taxes, state tax controversy resolutions, and credit taxes too. He understood long ago that numbers, like letters, were interpretable and malleable, dependent solely on perspective. His number two pencil swam through the test sheets.

Viet finished early. He pushed his chair back and stood

to leave. But when he thought about how desperately Huong wanted him to get this job, he sat down again, remembering what she'd said the first time they met. "The man of perfect virtue is cautious and slow in speech."

He was a first year professor and she was a student at the University. They were in line at a deli near campus and Viet was with his best friend, an economics professor. The best friend was talking too much trying to impress the co-ed while Viet remained quiet, not sure what to say. He was unnerved by Huong's beauty, the haunting eyes, the see-through skin, the blue of the veins on her wrists. And then those eyes turned to him, her mouth opened, and she quoted the Confucian saying. Years later, Huong confessed that she'd known all along that he was a philosophy professor, "the one rumored to be obsessive about the ancient Chinese."

Yet as he sat on the 29th floor of a downtown skyscraper looking down at the tiny dots below, Viet held on to the advice of the clever young flirt. He double-checked his answers. The remaining time he spent writing down his favorite Confucian anecdotes on the back of an old grocery receipt.

Back at the post office, his co-workers, "the crew," they liked to call themselves, stood over their bins sorting mail by zip code.

"Where you been, little guy?" asked David.

Viet nodded a hello. He had told David before that in his country younger persons greeted elders with respect but the boy either chose to ignore it or had already forgotten. Viet thought how embarrassing it must be, to throw about careless words and not even realize it.

Melvin said "What's up, little man?" and continued with his story. "Yep, like I was saying met me a sweet baby Saturday night." Viet stepped in and took the only bin available between the part-time student and the playboy.

"How sweet?" asked David.

Melvin paused and licked his lips. "So sweet, she was like unwrapped candy. Sugar and molasses spilling outta her unbuttoned shirt."

Viet felt sorry for the two women in the group. They were outnumbered and had to listen in on the talk of depraved men. One woman rolled her eyes and smacked her gum saying, "You're so gross, Melvin." But the other woman stepped forward. She blushed a guilty rouge color and wiped the steam from her glasses.

Perhaps I am too sensitive, Viet thought.

Viet didn't talk much because his English embarrassed him. His co-workers didn't ask much of him either. They told stories amongst themselves and whispered secrets he pretended he was oblivious to. He once heard a co-worker describe him by saying he was as "quiet as they come." They were talking in general terms about the droves of Asians they noticed arriving in San Francisco over the past few years. They noted how passive they were and quiet too and how Viet topped them all by being the quietest of all, practically invisible.

Viet realized that each person possessed his own hopes and fears. But every day, it was the same continual banter. One woman always talked about her unfaithful boyfriend. The other gushed about the celebrity gossip she read in the news. David talked about the Chevy Malibu he was fixing up and the places he'd go. Melvin talked about the girls, the endless line of anonymous bodies with interchangeable heads.

He let their words pass with the hours. It was like the French cargo planes of his youth, white noise so thunderously loud it became an indistinguishable drone. The postal work was tedious and Viet kept his mind alive by composing poems in his head for his daughters. During breaks, he'd write out the lines on scratch paper and then in the solitude of night when all the women in the house were sleeping, he recopied the poems on a linen scroll in calligraphy. He was saving them as wedding gifts for the girls.

At lunchtime that day, his oldest daughter strutted into the post-office. It upset him to see her, mid-day, out of class. She made a striking impression though, big smile and lithe limbs swinging. Elle had her waist length hair braided into cornrows. They pulled so tight on her scalp it gave her a feline-like appearance.

"Everything ok? Why you not in school?" Viet asked.

"Hi to you too, Dad." She was chewing bubble gum.

"Answer me." He paused to look over the braids, the blackness of it; decided she still looked pretty, refrained from comment.

"Mom asked me to bring you lunch today." She handed over a grocery-sized brown paper bag. She had recently turned thirteen and already stood his height. She leaned in and whispered, "How was your interview?"

"Good," he said, "good." He looked in the bag and saw a glass jar of homemade soymilk. There was also a Tupperware container with white rice and what looked like steak (and probably was because Huong always made his favorite dishes on special occasions). A fork and knife were rolled and rubber-banded in a paper-towel.

Melvin came up and said, "Viet, man, how come you never introduce me to your family before?"

"This my daughter, Elle," said Viet. He was about to tell his daughter that this was his co-worker, Melvin. But when Viet looked up, Melvin already had his hand reaching out at the girl. Melvin was smiling, all mouth, and big white teeth.

"Pleasure meeting such a beautiful young lady. I'm Melvin. You call me Mel, alright?" He winked.

She shook his hand and said, "Good meeting you, Mel." Then she stepped away, turned to Viet and said, "My friends are waiting outside."

Viet walked her to the doorway and watched her clicking down the halls, stirring up dead air with her swinging arms. Viet was in awe of his daughters, their quick minds, their ability to adapt in this new world. He admired their pliable female tongues that danced and twirled in a storm of lyrical English. He marveled at their grace and courage, forced to age beyond their years. His wife always lectured them, "Be thankful we made it here. In Vietnam, they don't even have food to eat."

In such moments, Viet often thought his daughters did nothing to deserve their adult mess, their ugly wars. It seemed to belittle the human spirit, to always be grateful that things could be worse. Of course he'd never speak these thoughts to Huong. She already thought he was too easy on the girls. Instead, he left Huong to her couch, with her remote control, vigilantly watching the twenty-four hour news channel, waiting for the next cruel blow to hit.

When Viet returned with his sure quiet steps, nobody noticed. Melvin was at it with another one of his stories. He said, "Shit, the girls be lovin' the Mel machine." Viet went about his last-minute chores. He barely listened while the other men surrounded Melvin with their eager attention. "Girls these days, might be lookin' like nice little schoolgirls but you know they be all nasty in the bed." The other men agreed, what with the make-up these girls wore, all done up, difficult to tell their age. Only young David rolled his eyes and mumbled something beneath his breath.

Viet put on his jacket and grabbed the can of stale

breadcrumbs for the birds he'd feed from the park bench across the street. He was about to leave when he heard, "That Elle, wouldn't mind having baby in bed."

Viet couldn't believe he heard his daughter's name come out of Melvin's mouth. "Who would've thought? Fine little thing coming outta…" Melvin continued on.

The room bulged. Viet's vision flattened out and grew fuzzy all at once. In his ears there was a sound like ball bearings rolling and grinding against each other. Viet grew so hot his fingertips burned. He could feel the wet between his toes. He held on to the back of a chair to brace himself. When he took a seat, the cool of the metal folding chair shocked him. He tried taking deep breaths and even imagined himself back in his living room doing *tai chi*. None of it helped. Viet put the can and the bag on the floor by his feet. He leaned over and massaged his temples. Over the roar, he heard the bragging baritone voice saying with a chuckle, "Then at the end, she said *Mel*, playing all sweet and cozy like."

Viet sized up the room. He looked at the sooty cloth bags bulging with mail, the bins overflowing with envelopes, and the dingy lockers. Melvin and his mouth stood exactly ten steps away. Viet counted. Melvin's foot rested on the wood bench in the center of the room. He was bent over with his elbow on his knee. The other men hovered around him like ants devouring dead debris. Viet picked up his lunch bag. Inside, the blade poked out from the paper towel.

Their boat had been drifting for a night and a day on the South China Sea. He was below deck with his youngest. They were molding rice balls with their palms and he was teaching her how to count. Already, his daughter was quick with numbers and he knew that by the end of the day, she'd be able to count to at least twenty-six for each of the mouths they had to feed.

She yelled "Twelve!" at the top of her lungs.

Viet reached over to pat her head just as the boat swayed forward and he lost his footing. "That must have been a big wave," he said. She giggled holding her belly but stopped when they heard a woman screaming overhead.

"Papa, what's that?"

A stampede of footsteps rushed to the side of the deck. "Shut up! Shut up!" The man spoke in a crude Vietnamese placing the emphasis on all the wrong vowels.

Viet put his finger to his lips. He kneeled down and placed a rice ball in her hand. "It's like playing hide-n-go-seek okay? Stay under this blanket until I come back for you." He kissed her forehead and closed the closet door.

Viet grabbed a knife and climbed the five steps knowing what he'd see before he even looked. Viet remembered his best friend, the brash economics professor warning, "It's suicide. Don't go. If the Communists don't catch you, you risk the boat sinking, if the boat doesn't sink, the pirates are there to kill you."

Through the hole of the rusted sheet metal Viet saw two men in shabby western dress. The taller one was unbearably thin. He wore bell-bottoms. His eyes were hidden behind a pair of mirrored aviator sunglasses and a mop of shaggy hair. He could have easily been one of Viet's students, languid, underfed, dreamy, with that fashionable look the girls were beginning to favor. Fashion boy shoved the families to the front and gestured with his knife like it was a wand. He yelled in his stilted Vietnamese, "Move! Faster! Faster!"

The shorter one looked like a bulldog with thick shoulders, a ferocious under-bite, and puffy eyelids. He wore a faded nicotine-white undershirt and brown pinstriped pants from the bottom half of a once nice suit. Viet couldn't identify their origin until the bulldog said, "We're never doing this again. We should have stopped. They have less and less, these fucking refugees." He spoke Chinese. Fashion boy was grinding his jaw at such a rate, Viet thought he'd wear his teeth down to a paste. The bulldog said, "Bitch, did you get high again?"

The short one was older and clearly the brains. He walked along the deck, assessing each passenger one by one. Finally, he picked old man Phuc. Viet thought, you fool let him go. He has nothing you'd want. Old man Phuc didn't care about money. He was a poet who'd fled his homeland with only a book of his own censored poems. He would read to the others at nightfall; memories of the Mekong, its dark fertile soil, and the pelican-like tides of schoolgirls in the the white *áo dài* from his youth. The old man had his arms raised in surrender when the bulldog slid the knife sweetly, gently, in a smooth line, as a warning slit across his throat.

When the blood rose and dripped down his collar, his wife finally broke through the crowd. "Take it," she cried and pulled down her pants. Beneath the roll of the old woman's pale belly and above her pubic mound, she had wrapped seven gold necklaces in a handkerchief, and duct-taped the couple's life savings on her pelvis.

Only two men and two knives and yet Viet knew why his friends didn't fight. They were boat people, half dead, no fight left, and so they dropped their gold and any fragments of hope into the dirty burlap sacks. The pirates moved through the crowd with ease. These families were already trained to lie down, close their eyes, take it, and wait for the abuse to pass.

When the men reached Huong, she took off her jacket and held it out by the collar. Viet thought, good girl, give them what they want. But the pirate stopped. He took his knife and pointed it at her chin. She covered her throat with her hand. He used his knife to wave her hand away. She dodged the blade but immediately slapped her hand back. Huong was covering the jade Buddha at the hollow of her throat.

The other passengers pleaded with her. "Forget it!" "Give it to him!" "Hand it over!"

Viet could hardly breathe. His fear tasted like a fist full of coins jammed in his mouth. He knew his wife wouldn't give him up the family heirloom without a fight. Instead she pushed her jacket into the bulldog's chest. With her hands she showed him the hard nuggets of gold and jewelry she had hand sewn into the quilted lining of the fabric.

The bulldog screamed at her until a wad of spit landed on her chin. Huong would later say he had horrible decaying breath and because she found this so foul she couldn't stop her tongue. "You are animals, dogs." She sneered in his face, "You rape the raped."

He didn't understand her, but he knew she'd cursed him. He grabbed her hair and shoved her face into the deck. The other passengers flinched. They all of course recognized Huong from the commercials of her modeling days. One man later recounted, "The thought of damaging that face was criminal."

From below, Viet watched as the bulldog yanked her pants and panties down to her knees. Huong struggled and kicked beneath him, but he had her pinned. When he pulled his pants down, his zipper got caught. The bulldog tried to free himself with just one hand so he could hold on to his blade.

Viet knew this moment was all he had. He found the spot to aim for, the jugular. He counted the man about eleven paces away but he was nervous because his eyesight was poor, his glasses were foggy, and his lenses were scratched from wedging his face against the rusted hole of the sheet metal door.

From the closet, his daughter whined, "Papa, I don't want to play anymore."

He said, "The game's almost over." Viet chanted over and over in his mind, *Strike first, strike first.* With his knife pressed against his thigh, he thought, if I fail my girls will lose not just one but two.

Viet tightened his grip on the blade handle, slid his other hand on the door knob, inhaled, exhaled, and finally pounced. Once outside, he attacked the bulldog from behind and snapped his chin back. The knife met resistance at first. Viet plunged in the blade. He worked it through and twisted it. The cut was deep and swift. The blood came flooding out.

Finding courage in the professor's bravery, the other men attacked the taller one. Fashion boy was so high he was practically defenseless despite his weapon.

Viet left the dead pirates on the deck, let the other men dispose of them, and went to retrieve Mai from the closet below deck.

Viet was the boat's official hero, but he retreated into silence.

Huong said, "You did the right thing. Why are you sad, Father?"

"I did the weak thing," he said. "It's easy to inflict harm. It takes nothing."

"You did it for us. Family," she said. Huong kissed his forehead and held him. She rocked him in her arms, her husband, who at home refused to kill a spider no matter how she begged. It too deserves life, he'd say before setting it free from his toilet paper grasp into her gardenia bushes.

Viet sobbed for days over the fragility of life, for the life he had taken, and the one he was given. He cried for having witnessed the weakness of men, who preyed on the innocent and the poor. He held his head in stained hands, believing he'd failed himself because he'd done the unthinkable and killed a **man.** He was common, crude as the rest, unable to live up to the non-violence he preached, wasn't the gentleman he always aspired to be.

Viet held his head in his hands. He had sweat stains under the armpits of his regulation short-sleeved postal shirt. His sack lunch was perched on his lap.

"She had her hair all braided up so you know she be liking the brothers," Melvin said carrying on.

Viet's heart had only had one desire and his body was moved to only one goal. *He needed to shut this man up.* He sat trembling with his entire arm hidden inside the brown grocery bag. Inside, he gripped the knife in his hand. David turned around, saw Viet, and signaled the others.

Melvin finally caught on. He said, "Damn Viet, why you be all eavesdropping and shit? Sitting there all quiet, man, I didn't know. Shit."

"You not a good man," Viet said his chin up. "My daughter, she thirteen-years-old, she a nice girl."

"I was only saying nice things about her, man. *Real nice.*"

A couple guys laughed under their breath, saying, Damn Melvin, you're a nut.

Viet stood up and the folding chair squeaked across the floor. He cradled the paper bag with one hand while the other still clutched the knife inside. "You disrespect her," he said. He felt the vein in the middle of his forehead pumping. It rushed blood to his ears. It brought him back to the emptiness of the seas, its violent waves. His vision swayed. But when he blinked and refocused, it was Melvin's eyes that he tracked. The black man's gaze stopped at Viet's shirt. It was so wet it was now transparent and Viet's ribbed undershirt showed through. Then the eyes moved to the brown paper bag and stayed there. They squinted, straining to understand what was inside. Viet tried to control his trembling and told himself; *shut him up, strike first, strike first.*

Melvin said, "I'm sorry, man."

Viet wouldn't let him finish. "You disrespect her," he said. "You talk about her, only thirteen, like whore." Viet found his amplified voice almost unrecognizable.

"Don't do nothing crazy," Melvin said.

"You disrespect me!"

"I was just foolin' around but I shouldn't a been talking like that." Melvin held his hands up in front of his chest, palms out. "Don't be mad now, come on."

Viet whispered it again; you disrespect *me*, beneath his breath, and exhaled before letting go of the knife.

Melvin, arms wide-open said, "I like you, you a cool little cat. I didn't mean nothin'. I swear. I didn't mean no disrespect."

"You see her again, you apologize," Viet said, dropping the bag.

The glass jar cracked at his feet. The soymilk leaked through the brown paper. Nobody noticed. Their eyes were fixed on big Melvin's arms wrapped around Viet, hugging him tight.

"Next time, just tell me to shut up al'right?" Melvin laughed. Smothered in Melvin's overly jovial embrace of brotherhood, Viet remembered a Confucian saying and repeated it in his head. *Don't worry if people don't recognize your merits; worry that you may not recognize theirs.*

Melvin slapped him on the back and said, solemn and concerned, "Man, why don't you come with us today? Chill with the boys." Viet felt foolish looking down at his brown shoes and the soggy corners of the brown bag. He was thankful for their easy forgiveness, but declined. He wanted more than anything to sit alone, at the bench with the birds, and eat his lunch quietly.

A MAP BACK TO THE WORLD
AND INTO YOUR HEART

Viet sat cross-legged beneath a weak sliver of sun on the edge of the carpet that divided his living room from the linoleum of the kitchen floor. He was hunched over a cutting board dicing jicama for his wife's meatballs. Sheets of newspaper were spread beneath and around him to avoid getting food bits on the brown carpeting. A gray skullcap was pulled low over his large ears. His wife and daughters wore theirs too, matching red for the two girls and Huong's hat matched his gray one since they had been on sale, two-for-one at Sears.

His oldest daughter Elle begged, "Can't we please turn on the heat?"

Huong said, "It's on."

"Can we turn it up then? You can't even feel it." The girls were on the sofa with the tops of their red caps touching and their feet hanging over on opposite ends of the armrests. They were watching MTV. It was a free two-week trial period and the girls devoured it.

"For goodness sakes put on another sweater. And socks!" Huong's gray hat stooped over the girls. She wrapped her hand around Elle's bare foot. "No wonder!" she said. "Use your head, those music videos are making your brains mushy. Maybe we should turn that noise off."

Huong passed by, reached down, cradled the bowl of jicama in her arm, and without a word sauntered back to the kitchen.

Elle reached her arms above her head in a manner so perfectly formed and agile, it reminded him of the Separating the Clouds *tai chi* posture that was part of his practice. She shook her younger sister's shoulders and ordered, "C'mon hurry, go get it."

Michelle did as told, obeying the pecking order of siblings. She sprinted. Her favorite rock band was performing. When Michelle was out of earshot, Viet said to his eldest, "You could have gone yourself. She likes them more than you. Remember to be nice."

Elle said, "Dad, nice guys finish last."

He didn't see Elle's face but knew she rolled her eyes when she said this. Her sass was bewildering given how close they used to be.

His wife said, "Watch your tone young lady."

Viet looked down at the chopping block and smiled inwardly. Huong's rare defense of him and loving attention felt like a warm wave washing down his spine. The feeling didn't last long because in her next breath she said, "My god, I asked you to *finely* dice the jicama and you give me these chunks big enough to chip a tooth on."

Viet joined his daughters on the couch. On the screen, men with make-up and frosted hair wiggled their hips to a crowd of adoring women. Huong was pounding away at the jicama with a cleaver.

She asked, "When will you hear back about that accounting job?"

"Tomorrow or the next day."

Viet could hardly understand what they were singing over the hysteria of screaming fans and electric guitars. The camera scanned the audience and in the crowd a girl who looked Elle's age had tears streaming down her pink face as she mouthed along to the words of a song she knew by heart. The lead singer had large blue wide spread eyes and pillow lips the color of strawberries. He was pretty in a calendar girl way. It made Viet squirm in his seat.

Huong said, "How many resumes did you send out last week?"

Viet nudged his daughters, "Which one is your favorite?"

"Him," they chimed in unison, signaling the lead. No surprise. Everything was reversed in this country. Even his daughters weren't immune.

Huong said, "Did you hear me?" and set the cleaver down.

"Three," said Viet. "I sent out three."

The pounding started again.

After dinner, Huong said she would retire to bed early. She said she was exhausted from the workweek. In fact, she hadn't slept well the entire week. The sight of the messy house made her even more tired.

Viet cleared Huong's bowl and chopsticks from the table. She had her hands on the table's edge and was about to push her chair out when she looked down at her dainty hands as if noticing them for the first time. "Remember when they used to be pretty? Now I have man hands."

He said, "Rest. We'll be quiet, right girls?" He smiled at Huong but she didn't catch it. She was still studying her hands, the backs and the fronts of them. She sighed loud enough for the entire family to hear as she disappeared into the bedroom.

Viet stood at the sink and stared at the pile of dishes. The girls spread out their homework on the kitchen table. They liked to be near him when they did math so that they could utter just one syllable, "Dad?," and help was a step away.

Outside, the night sky was crisp and clear. It was an unusual San Francisco evening with the stars outshining the fog and the glare of the city lights. From the kitchen window, Viet looked out at the half moon and beside it he glimpsed Pisces, Huong's astrological sign. Viet loved the night sky. He liked its ability to calm him and the sense of order it imposed.

From the corner of his eye, he was delighted to see the bottom half of Princess Andromeda. When he craned his neck and stood on tiptoes, he could make out the entirety of the poor Chained Lady.

"Come take a look." He waved the girls over. One by one, he held each girl up to the window and told them Andromeda's story. He recounted how the Queen's vanity caused the Princess to be banished away until in the end, luckily, Perseus saved her.

Elle said, "Maybe that's why when someone says we're cute mom always has to say, 'Well, they're not *too* ugly.'"

Michelle added, "I hate that."

Viet said, "You know your mom thinks you're pretty. You both look like her. But it's important to remember the Princess' story because it's a lesson in humility. It's not nice to brag."

After the stargazing, Viet returned to the dishes. In Vietnam, he had never even washed a plate. Growing up, his father didn't allow the boys to do women's work. Once married, Viet and Huong kept a maid. Yet now he had become a dishwashing expert. He used the soft soapy side of the sponge for the ceramic and plastic surfaces. He even knew not to squeeze the liquid soap directly on the sponge but rather to mix it in a bowl with warm water because it went further that way. He let the pans soak to later scrub down with steel wool. Maybe restaurant work was the next job he should apply for.

Viet had been unemployed for eight months. The post office suggested he take a temporary leave after he had a disagreement with a co-worker. There were rumors that people feared he might go "postal." Soon enough, the temporary leave turned permanent.

He had never been out of work before. Even in their first months in America, he worked a short stint as a gardener on an almost all-Mexican crew. All day he would see mailmen strolling out in the sunshine up and down the hills. In this beautiful new city, it seemed everywhere you looked there was something wonderful to see. From Pacific Heights, you could see views of Alcatraz and Angel Island. From the Presidio you saw the majestic sweep of the Golden Gate Bridge. Even from Chinatown, a person could glimpse the powerful peak of the TransAmerican building. That's when Viet got the idea to apply for the postal service job. He worked as a mailman in the day and attended night school in the evenings.

Because everyone said, "Computers are the wave of the new generation," he completed a computer programming certification. But it yielded no luck. Employers wanted young whiz kids from universities for these positions. After that, Viet went back to the local state college to get a Bachelor of Science in Accounting. He walked chin high with cap and gown fluttering across the auditorium stage. His hope had wings back then. His newly earned accounting degree, along with his law degree and his PhD in philosophy from Vietnam would certainly assure a stable job. But the failed job interviews, one after another, proved him wrong. In the end, it was Huong's certification from Heald College and her job as an electronics assembler that allowed her to feed the family.

Viet stood at the sink and thought, what's fair is fair. If she's "bringing home the bacon," (a term he had learned in ESL) then he had to help around the house. He soaped a bowl with a chip on its rim. He gently sponged around a plate's hairline crack. He rinsed a teacup with a missing handle. They were the casualties from his first months of unemployment.

"Dad?" Elle looked up at him with pleading eyes. "This one's impossible, check it out." She pushed her textbook in his direction.

She had her mother's eyes. His friends used to describe them as doe-like, but to Viet it was the luminous underwater quality that made them special. They made you feel like you were swimming. When Huong was utterly focused on you, it could feel like a seductive dream. He missed this most. It had been so long since they were last intimate.

Viet snapped the dishrag over his shoulder. "Let me at it," he said with a wink.

In the morning, Viet woke to the smell of fresh coffee brewing. He was wiping the lenses of his glasses on the bottom half of his shirt and tripped over Huong in the kitchen. She was on her hands and knees swiping up dust bunnies from the floor with dampened toilet tissue.

"You're up early," he said.

"I swear to you, I'm taking those girls to Super Cuts next weekend." Huong held up a tangle of hair and dust. "You should have seen how much hair I picked up from the carpet. It's so stubborn, the vacuum won't suck it up." She said matter-of-factly, "That's why I cut mine off."

Last month, Huong walked through the front door, set her purse down on the counter, the groceries on the kitchen floor, and said, "What do you feel like for dinner?" She acted as if nothing had changed although her head was completely shorn.

Viet had been wondering why she cut off her hair but hadn't asked, fearing it might hurt her feelings.

His wife was stunning with long hair; with her height, and high cheekbones, and those big eyes that were sometimes covered just at the slightest angle by the sheen of raven hair, she was a knock out. Her short hair took a bit of getting used to, but Huong was lucky, she had the features to pull it off. She was still a handsome woman and he still reached for her in the night forgetful in his half-sleep that in this new chapter of their lives she would inevitably turn away.

Now she shook her impish head and dropped the garbage into the trash bin. As the toilet paper fluttered from her fingertips, Viet noticed her wedding ring glinting in the sun. The sight of it jolted him. She hadn't worn it for years. As soon as she started on the assembly line she had declared, "It's impractical to wear in a place like that." Viet poured himself a cup of coffee.

She said, "Look, you dripped," pointed to the lone drop of coffee, and attacked it with a sponge. He watched her coasting from appliance to appliance wiping all available surfaces. Huong buzzed around the kitchen from toaster to blender to microwave. "I hate messiness." She scrunched up her face, causing her button nose to twitch like a kitten. "It's disgusting."

Meanwhile, Viet was following the diamond as it glided through the air. Huong's hummingbird reflexes led him to see tracers. He blinked, gulped down the rest of his coffee, and once he gained his lucidity asked, "Why are you wearing it?" He caught hold of her left hand and squeezed it. For a moment, they both looked down at the ring before she slipped out of his reach.

"Why not? It's pretty, don't you think?" She talked into her shoulder while walking away.

Viet didn't understand it. His wife was far too practical a creature to wear a diamond ring while assembling circuit boards. He heard his daughters stumbling awake. A deep voice from a morning talk show crackled from the bedroom radio. The old apartment pipes grumbled and then the showerhead roared. A brief bickering session between the sisters was just as quickly followed by a tide of giggles. He began packing the girls their bag lunches.

Even after everyone was gone and he was left alone in the stillness of the apartment, the ring continued to preoccupy him. Most men would be happy their wives wore their wedding rings. But why had Huong suddenly cut her hair and now this?

Viet tried to push it aside. He had more important things to worry about. He went to grab the day's paper from the doorstep. Outside, the sky was defeated, the color of a trapped sun unable to break through. It was so cold, the usual loiterers on his front step found refuge indoors. Across the street, a gang of boys whizzed by on bicycles. Dark hoods covered their faces and they reminded Viet of a stampede of antelopes on the savannah. He liked the sight of their wild freedom on the barren streets.

At the kitchen table, he spread out the paper, poured himself another cup of coffee, and uncapped his red pen. Hopefully, today's classifieds would include new listings he was qualified for.

He was flipping to the Job Opportunities section, when his eyes glanced over a section called the Personals where people were seeking people. *Blue eyes, slim figure, seeking single man for dating/ Honest man 41 years young seeking Honest woman with matrimony as objective.* There were all sorts of requests and preferences but what struck Viet were the disproportionate ads requesting Asian women in particular. *Wealthy mature man seeking young Asian lovely for companionship and travel/ Swinging couple curious for Oriental affec-*

tion/ Modeling opportunity for hot geisha babes.

He found it peculiar that an American city would hold such high demand for a minority race. He wondered if it was simple math and actually proportionate. Perhaps there were more Asians in San Francisco than whites. At least when he delivered in neighborhoods like the Sunset and Chinatown it seemed true. And then it hit him, clear as day.

Viet suddenly understood what Huong was doing with the haircut and then the wedding ring. She was trying to protect him, their marriage. She wore it as an effort to ward off other men. A flood of emotion rose in Viet's throat. The lump made him choke as he reached for his coffee. He gulped it without thinking and burned his tongue.

He had witnessed the way men stole furtive glances at her when they went grocery shopping, rode the bus, walked in the park with the girls. Surely, some of these men had greater means than he.

His mind wandered. Maybe she had already committed adultery. Maybe the co-worker she had cheated with wouldn't leave her alone and now she wore the ring as a sign. Maybe she was copying the Buddhist nuns. They shaved their heads to show a shedding of worldly desires. Maybe Huong was now repenting her sin.

In the end, Viet knew it was nonsense. His wife was a beautiful, worrywart, insomniac, who worked hard and had a temper and still he knew he was lucky to have her. Today's revelation was more proof of the greatness of that heart she attempted to confine in her crab shell.

To show his gratitude, Viet decided that he was going to clean the entire apartment, from top to bottom. He flipped on the TV for background noise to keep himself company. The girls last had it in on the music video channel and again that same rock band shimmying in tight clothes and big hair serenaded him. In America it appeared there was nothing wrong with a man exploring his yin side.

Viet dedicated the most time to the kitchen. They spent the majority of their time as a family in this room. He scrubbed down the stovetop, cleaned the oven, mopped the floors, and even cleaned out the refrigerator, which included wiping up some caked up spills that had built up several tenants ago. It took up the entire morning.

By noon, Viet had moved on the bathroom. He was in the tub on all fours with nothing on but some yellow rubber gloves when the doorbell rang. In haste, Viet grabbed his wife's silky canary yellow robe from the back of the bathroom door and tied it on.

The young man outside said, "Hi, I'm here for your free carpet cleaning appointment?"

Viet said, "There must be a mistake, I didn't make an appointment." He hid behind the door and cracked it just enough to reveal his face and his steamed up glasses that had slid down the bridge of his nose.

The young man said, "Don't worry sir, it's free. You just pick any one room you want me to clean and that's it. Deal?" The man took a step forward and stuck out his hand. He had blonde hair neatly parted and combed to the side. He had what Viet considered all-American good looks, the kind of person Viet could imagine in commercials selling toothpaste and cereal.

Viet thought, what a lucky coincidence and opened the door. The man let himself and his equipment in. When he realized what Viet was wearing, his eyes nervously darted around the apartment. Viet said, "No, no, this is my wife's," and wrapped the robe around a notch tighter.

"I just came out here from Wyoming. People are a lot more easy going out here I guess." The man had a slight twang to his voice. He wore an ironed white shirt and even ironed his jeans. A crease ran the length of his long legs. He had cowboy boots on underneath. His tall lankiness looked out of place in their box of an apartment. He said, "Point me to the room sir."

Viet took him to the living room. He was going to return to the tub when the man insisted that Viet observe the cleaning. Viet felt silly sitting on the couch in a thin woman's robe, watching a stranger clean his living room, but he believed it was well worth it. A professional carpet cleaning with shampoo usually cost at least thirty dollars.

The young man unpacked shiny heavy looking metal parts from a large cardboard box. "My name's Troy," he said. He was assembling the vacuum and fitting a hose into the canister. "Bear with me, almost got her going for you here." His tongue poked out from the side of his mouth as he concentrated on putting the machine together. "The other guys do this in a couple of minutes. I'm pretty new at this. I'm used to live things bucking at me, ya know? I used to ride in the circuit back home." Troy said he was a cowboy from a ranching family that had hit hard times. He mumbled something about "globalization."

Viet understood that cowboys were a dying breed and instantly felt a bond with the young man. He asked, "Can I offer you some green tea?"

Troy presented what he called a Kirby vacuum, and said it was the best in its class. He replaced the vacuum bag with a clear plastic chamber that allowed you to watch the dirt being sucked through. He also produced some white filters that you could pull from the chamber in order to look at the dirt up close.

"Why don't you pull out your vacuum so we can compare," said Troy. Viet pulled out his red Hoover upright from the hall closet. He ran it across the carpet in just one spot a couple of times as directed by Troy and then sat back down on the couch. Troy then went over the exact same spot with the shiny chrome and steel of the Kirby. Sure enough he was able to extract an entire pile of dirt and sand. Troy continued to change filter after soiled filter, cleaning 10 different spots on the carpet.

"This here motorized vacuum head cost $29 million dollars for NASA to develop. That's why it's so good. You've got all-American NASA engineering." Viet nodded at the staggering statistics. Troy said, "How much do you think something like this costs?"

"Five hundred dollars?"

Troy said, "The vacuum sells for $1,550 to $1,800 depending on the upgrades you choose. But wait, I have a lot more to show you."

The two men stood over the couch and Troy used the upholstery attachment on the cushions. Troy said, "You'll never believe the kind of filth you've been rollin' around in." He pulled out a black filter this time. It created a sharp contrast with the white debris he sucked out, what he declared to be "dust mite poop and dead skin." "Ugh," he said, and made a face like he was going to retch.

Viet knew he wanted it when Troy said he might be able to lower the price to $1200 as a special offer today only. When Troy asked to use the house phone to call his boss and see if he could get an even better price, Viet tried to look calm on the outside, but inside, he was excitedly holding his breath. After Troy hung up, he announced that he could sell the vacuum for just "$995, payable on a five-year payment plan."

Viet looked over at the pile of dust filters stacked with soot and soil in the corner of the room. The sight of it sickened him. After everything he had sacrificed to come to this country, he couldn't have his family living in this kind of filth. He decided, "Ok, it's a deal."

Viet filled out the paper work. He asked Troy to leave the soiled filters out. He wanted to show Huong the power of this machine. He knew it was expensive, but he had a good feeling about the most recent accounting interview. Besides, Huong was always complaining what a shame it was that they had to leave behind all the items of value they used to own in Vietnam. This he determined would be a true quality purchase and an item they could use for the rest of their lives.

The demonstration had taken up over an hour of his afternoon. After Troy left, Viet rushed back to the tub. He wanted to finish the bathroom with enough time to foam clean both bedroom carpets with the new Kirby before Huong returned.

When the girls came home from school, the apartment was spotless. For the finishing touches Viet had watered the plants, misted Huong's indoor herb box, and even dusted. He had debated whether he should leave the Kirby out on display or put it away to later pull out for the sake of showmanship and surprise. He opted for the latter.

He was giddy with excitement and expected the girls to comment on the polish of the apartment, but they didn't.

Michelle said, "I'm hungry, Dad," as she plopped down at the kitchen table with her backpack still on her back. Her long hair was caught in the straps of her bag.

Viet said, "One thing at a time," and swept her hair out from beneath the backpack while unharnessing her.

Elle said, "Can you fry up the *lop choeng*?"

Viet asked, "Do you notice anything different?"

They looked him over and Michelle asked, "Did you get a haircut, Dad?"

"I cleaned all day today." He waved his hand like a magician in the air pointing all around.

They glanced around and Elle said, "It does look nice," nodding in concession.

He knew they were kids and didn't notice details but he couldn't resist. Viet swung open the closet door to show them the Kirby. "Take a look at this," he said.

They didn't seem overly enthused.

Michelle eyed the red Hoover, "Did that other vacuum break or something?"

Then Elle asked, "How much did it cost? Was it expensive?"

His spirits fell. He said, "You can split a package of Top Ramen but I'm not frying up the Chinese sausage. It's greasy and I don't want to stink up the place and ruin the surprise after all my hard work."

Huong came home, dropped her purse on the floor and ran to the bathroom. It wasn't the romantic homecoming he had envisioned. From the bathroom, she said, "Wow, the bathroom is so clean. Did you clean? It smells lemony in here."

He stood on the other side of the door with his arms crossed. He heard the roll of the toilet paper and then her flush. "I just thought the place needed a touch up," he said with a self-satisfied smile on his face.

She came out and fixed her eyes on him. Her gaze held steady for the first time in months. "That was nice," she said. Huong went to kitchen, greeted the girls, and opened the fridge. She held the refrigerator door steady and the ring winked at him from across the room. Her rump was in the air and her head was inside the fridge and even after fifteen years of marriage, he still felt a deep carnal stirring for her.

She said, "Maybe we can make something special for dinner tonight. Let's steam that sea bass. And how about we fry up the lop choeng to go with some fried rice."

The girls' ears perked up like rabbits when they heard this. Michelle said, "We asked for the Chinese sausage earlier but Dad wouldn't let us. He said it would make the house stinky and ruin his surprise for you." At this, Huong turned to Viet and smiled her closed-mouth girlish smile. His heart leapt.

Elle said, "If someone has a surprise, you're not supposed to tell them they're getting a surprise stupid." She rolled her eyes at Michelle.

Huong said, "The cleaning was surprise enough. There's more?"

Michelle said, "A present. Go look!" She pointed down the hallway.

Huong said, "I don't want a present. We can't afford any presents."

Viet hurriedly crossed the kitchen, went down the hallway and said, "Follow me." He then opened the closet door, pulled out the Kirby, and with a flourish of his wrist said, "Voila!"

Huong crossed her arms. With utter disapproval she said, "I know that's not for me because I already own a vacuum."

Viet said, "But you should see it go."

She continued, "Plus, it's winter and I can't even afford to turn on the heat so I know real American dollars weren't spent on that thing. Especially, *especially* when my husband hasn't been working for a year."

Viet was uncoiling the cord to plug in the power.

Huong asked, "How much was it?"

Viet had asked Troy for a couple of clean white filters. He had planned on replicating the demonstration for Huong. But he didn't even have a chance to switch on the Kirby because she erupted the second she heard the price.

Much later that evening, after Huong retired to bed without

eating and the girls were tucked away, Viet sat alone in the stillness of the night staring at the soiled dust filters he had forgotten to show her. They were spread out on the kitchen table like a constellation of stars. Each time he moved a filter, the debris would fall off and leave a trail not unlike the gaseous particles of the moon or a planetary ring. Huong had used ugly words before, "useless, good for nothing, unemployed." But the most hurtful came from Elle, when his fourteen-year-old daughter said in a voice trembling with defeat, "See, I told you, nice guys finish last."

In his youth, Viet had naively believed that he held the world in his hands. Orion, Pleiades, Pegasus, the winged horse soaring away. He shuffled the stars in different patterns, looking for a map into the world, a direction to follow, the way back to her heart.

SILVER GIRL

On the Fourth of July we glide through the winding roads of Mt. Tam with the top down. Tree tops sway and leaves shimmer like tinsel when the moon hits just right. Over the railing the Pacific Coast is as placid as a lake tonight. Phoebe's dad takes the curves hard and fast. He pumps even harder when Aretha Franklin goes off on her scat. Her lungs are like the gale winds of the Bay. But still Stan puts the music loud. He's a jazz musician. He plays trumpet. He's deaf in one ear from his years next to a speaker.

Phoebe and I are squeezed together in the front bucket seat. We're bundled up in matching sweaters and blue jeans and scream with the turns of our stomachs. We're hunched over with the heat high. Our noses nestled against the vents, cheeks touching. We like the hot-cold look of reddened cheeks, chapped lips, the wind through our hair. We like how it feels even better. Phoebe's dad says we're complicated women. Already we groove on contradiction. I like being called a woman. My father would call us kids.

My father would say, roll up the windows and turn off the heat. He would say, either-or, why both? My father's at home tonight. He's bathing in the blue light of his sitcoms. His bared feet are crossed at the ankles, propped up on the coffee table. He's rubbing them together when he says, "Sure you don't want to stay home with us? Michelle is helping mom make *pho*. Aunt Kim and Sophia are coming over. We can all watch the fireworks on TV." His two big toes are bruised from cheap shoes, steep hills, the weight of the world on his back.

At the top of the mountain Stan parks on a dirt shoulder. Phoebe and I run to the cliff's edge. She screams, "Come on Elle! Last one to the wall…" I'm sprinting fast, lungs full, out of breath. Beyond us, the city lights beckon. The sprawling hills stretch until they roll underwater. I imagine swimming in a sea of silver stars.

Phoebe is ahead of me spinning and pirouetting, jumping so high she defies gravity. My best friend looks like those princesses they draw in children's fairy tales. She has sweet clear eyes and Botticelli lips and a blaze of auburn hair always in perfect disarray from riding in her dad's convertible. The top of her head skims the tip of a maple leaf and for a fleeting moment she is crowned. I watch afraid if I blink she might disappear forever.

Last month, on the last day of junior high, we pricked our fingers and swore we'd remain Bo Diddley and Wonder Woman, soul sisters forever. Come September she'll be starting high school at the School of the Arts. For now we pretend that the summer will be endless, that the fall will never arrive.

When I told my parents I wanted to go to SOTA, too, they said we couldn't afford it.

I said, "But it's public and free."

My father said, "But it's not practical."

I said, "But what happens if I get in?"

My father changed the channel. The remote is wrapped in plastic. It is like everything in our house.

Phoebe and I lean on the wall. The moss is cool. It tickles

our elbows. We can see the entire peninsula, all five bridges. We call out their names: the Golden Gate and the Bay Bridge, the Richmond and the San Mateo. Our words bounce back in the wind. Way out in the distance we can see the Dumbarton too. That's how clear it is tonight. It's so far away it looks like a stray piece of string.

From the car, Aretha is belting out a gospel. She sounds like a velvet storm you could drown in. Phoebe calls to Stan but his head is buried in the trunk. She rolls her eyes and says, "At least your dad isn't always in his own world."

I remember the first time I spent the night at their house. Stan came home and started playing the piano at one in the morning. He sounded like Chet Baker singing "Smoke Gets in Your Eyes," with a voice so timid it trembled. He was tapping his foot and because the piano bench had a wobbly leg it added an extra beat against the hardwood floors. He nodded at us and then at the wide open windows and the moonlight. His tweed bowler hat tipped over his brow. Phoebe screamed, "Come on Dad! Don't you know the time?" A breeze swept through and flapped the calendar pages on the wall. Stan grinned and played on. I couldn't help it, I grinned too.

My father doesn't like sleepovers. He says no proper girl would ever spend the night away, or even want to for that matter. As punishment, he sits me down with a date book. "High school's next year and every minute counts." Six to seven—swim practice. Seven to eight—breakfast with flashcards. After school, violin lessons from four to five. Five to six—French tutor. Six to seven—dinner. Seven to nine—homework. Nine to ten—relax. "You're scheduling in a relax hour?"

"When else would you do it?" he asks. He picks up the remote. *Three's Company* is on tonight. It's his favorite show. He laughs along with the laugh track. Stan calls it a laugh trap.

Stan slams the trunk and its tinny echo slices through the warmth of the night. When he approaches I can still hear the music play. It's muffled but I can tell it's Aretha singing, "Bridge Over Troubled Water."

Stan catches my eye and says, "Hey silver girl."

Phoebe says, "If she's silver girl, who am I?"

He says, "You're gold."

My father once told me about the ancient Kingdom of Angkor Wat. How the royal family sprinkled gold dust on themselves. How they were seen by their public only one night of the year, on the eve of the harvest moon. Their naked bodies glowed beneath firelight and when the embers died, they vanished. The villagers thought they were gods. I wondered what it was like for them the rest of the year. My father is filled with these tidbits on history and religion. He used to be a philosophy professor back in Vietnam. Now he says, "Lofty ideas are a luxury of the rich."

Phoebe glances at the paper bag cradled in Stan's arm and asks, "What took so long?" He hops up and sits on top of the wall. We copy him and climb on too, me on one side, Phoebe on the other. Our legs hang over the ledge. I know my father wouldn't approve. He says teasing death is only fun when you don't know what it smells like.

The tree tops below our feet look like baby broccoli heads. I ask, "Did you pack sandwiches in there?" We haven't had dinner yet.

Stan sets his brown bag down. He says, "I'm not hungry. But we can get food on the way back." He flicks his cigarette butt. When I kick it the red ashes spray.

He says, "What d'ya know, those are practically fluorescent in the moonlight."

Phoebe says, "Her dad polishes her sneakers. And guess who

did her hair?"

I say, "It's just because I can't reach the back by myself."

Phoebe says, "Dad, you've never helped me curl my hair."

"You've never asked."

"No," she says, "it's because when Kristen was around I wasn't allowed more than fifteen minutes in the bathroom."

The first night Stan met Phoebe's soon-to-be step mom, he came home craving his deceased mother's *puttanesca*. It didn't matter that it was around midnight and he had to wake us up. I chopped tomatoes. Phoebe diced onions. And while Stan minced the anchovy fillets this was the story he told.

He'd been in Sausalito at his regular Saturday night gig at a place everyone called the No Name because it literally had no name. "There's no sign, just a door," he said. You push through a heavy wooden block and then you're in an open air bar like an old-fashioned Spanish courtyard. "I've never really dug blondes before," he said, "but..." But maybe it was how the bar had white Christmas lights hanging from the trees and she looked like a little angel with her platinum hair framing her face in wisps. Or maybe it was how she drank Shirley Temples one after another. Or how even from the stage he could see that she was shivering. He said to me, "She's practically your size."

During the break he grabbed his jacket and offered it to her. Up close she had the saddest eyes he'd ever seen. They were "bewitching." He said her name, "Kristen," and then repeated it again in a reverent whisper. I promised on the spot that one day a man would say my name with that much awe. "That one's gonna break my heart," he said, "but I don't care."

We played Sinatra records and rolled up the rug and Phoebe and I took turns letting Stan spin us on the hardwood floors and out to the deck and then down to the grass where the dew was sticky between my toes. In the lilac hours of daylight, the sheets pulled up to my chin, I dreamt about the shimmy and women who looked like angels, and the promise of flight.

Tonight Stan denies Kristen's spell. He's pretending things didn't change when she came around. "That's hogwash," he says, "Baloney!"

I'm so hungry I can hear my stomach growl. At my house my parents shove food down your throat the second you walk through the door. If you don't eat anything, they'll put a papaya in your backpack or give you some persimmons to take home to your parents.

At Phoebe's house we eat at odd hours and drink coffee. We sit in the shadows of the living room where it's dark and musty and smells like old wood and roasted coffee and we listen to Stan's jazz albums. He makes coffee drinks from his fancy Italian espresso machine while we write down "the vibe" we get from the song. "How's the piano talking to the sax? What are the sounds saying to you?" Stan encourages us to express ourselves.

Phoebe and Stan live in Noe Valley in a real house where the sun shines and there's a backyard that smells of jasmine. We live in a box in the fog of the Richmond district squished between other boxes. My father doesn't like that I'm always staying the night away. "Is there something wrong with our home?" He tells me that in Vietnam, the word "sleepover" doesn't exist.

I say words like "privacy" and "passion" aren't in the Vietnamese language either. "Does that mean they don't exist?"

"You're getting mouthy," he says. "See what the sleepovers are doing to your attitude?" I like that "mouthy" is used the same way in English and in Vietnamese. Finding these connections helps me feel better.

I've started writing. Mostly it's nonsense. I use the things littered on Phoebe's living room floor as paper. I write on grocery bags and pizza boxes, candy wrappers and cigarette packs. I make lists. Stone, beat, dark.

The only present Stan ever gave me was a journal. It had a red leather cover with thick crisp paper inside. "Copy this down for me will ya?" He gave me a pizza box I'd written a poem on. He said he might make it into a song.

I came home and asked my parents, "Why don't we talk more?"

My father said, "We talk plenty." He switched back to the TV.

One day I said, "We watch too much TV."

My father said, "But we watch TV to improve our English. You said you wanted us to talk more."

My parents understand practical functional English. They have learned the English of ESL, the language of getting from A to B, questions, commands, directions, a job in a new country. They speak in the language of survival. We are boat people, refugees. Sometimes when we talk it's as if we're drifting apart at sea.

My father's diplomas from Vietnam are water stained. There is a PhD in philosophy and a law degree too. They're yellowing and hanging on the wall above the TV. In contrast, beside them are the new bright white diplomas from America. He went to night school and earned a computer-programming certificate. After that, he got a BS in Accounting too. My father believes education is the ticket out. He says you can choose to be a doctor. They help others and are respected in society. He says you can choose to be an engineer. Decent paycheck and math comes easy to you. He says be a professor, excellent benefits and the students will keep you young.

Phoebe's dad says, "Follow your passion."

Out toward the East, Stan points to the hydraulic boatlifts

and says, "George Lucas was sitting right here looking out at 'em when he got the idea for the ATs-ATs in *The Empire Strikes Back*." The boatlifts look mystical and foreboding, rising out from the sea like post-industrial dragons. Although I've heard some people call them dinosaurs and others call them Dobermans, I know them as guardians. They stand at attention on the edge of the coast. They're perched and ready, here to protect the inhabitants of the Bay. If my parents knew this maybe they wouldn't stay tucked inside their apartment all the time, hidden behind two deadbolts and a squeaky screen door.

Stan once played a gig at the Lucas Ranch estates. He was instructed to wear a tux and bring a blindfold. Kristen didn't like the idea of him going alone. She said that if Stan loved her he would sneak her in. She could pretend to be a backup dancer. "It could be my big break," she said. When Stan said it was out of his hands, Kristen said, "Everything slips through your hands." She squeezed hers into tight fists. The biceps she'd gained from teaching her Taut-N-Tone classes bulged.

Later that night, Phoebe overheard Kristen saying she was too young to have given up her acting career for him and for a daughter who wasn't even hers. That's when Phoebe told me about the survey. They did a survey where they asked a bunch of people, if you were on a sinking ship and you could only save either your spouse or your child, who would you pick? Ninety percent of the women chose the kid and ninety percent of the men chose the wife.

Phoebe asked, "Elle, who would your father choose?"

Stan balances on one arm, lifts his hips off the wall, and fumbles for his back pocket. Phoebe says, "Careful, you're scaring me." He pulls out a corkscrew and uncorks the bottle from his bag.

The day before Kristen left, we had a big barbeque in their

back yard with his sponsor and her sponsor and all of their other AA friends to celebrate Stan's two-year chip. We grilled fish and shrimp, tofu and tempeh burgers. Phoebe and I volunteered to circulate with the trays of sushi. The coolers were all iced up brimming with Calistogas and Martinelli's, sodas and juices. Stan and Kristen seemed happy, arms around each other, all kisses and affection. (I'd never seen my parents hug). But the very next day, Kristen's leotards and leg warmers and her rainbow array of high top sneakers were all packed into her duffel bags and gone. Since then Stan's been drinking again. He's barely picked up his trumpet. He doesn't even finish his scales before going off for yet another drive.

Phoebe and Stan are talking about the *Star Wars* movies and she asks, "Dad, do you think I'm pretty enough to be an actress?"

He says, "You'd rule the world hon, if you didn't let your own fears get in the way."

Phoebe is looking into the night sky, dreaming stars and smiling. She says, "I wonder when the fireworks will start." They're huddled together and she puts her head on his shoulder. It is silent all around except for the chirring of crickets. It sounds like escaping in the middle of the night. It is the sound of hope and fear stuffed so deep it coos.

My father says, "Elle, your mother and I risked our lives to come here. I know you'll make us proud. I know you'll care for us when we're old." He massages his feet. He soaks them in a big pot of warm water and sits back on the couch. Often he'll ask me, "How did I get reincarnated from a man to a mule all in a lifetime? Why go on at all?"

A warm wind passes and we sigh. We can see out past the Marin Headlands and then the very faint beam from the lighthouse on Angel Island. Right beside the old Russian forts is the island prison of Alcatraz. Beyond it is San Quentin and Stan just stares. He takes small sips and closes his eyes after each one.

He swigs from his bottle and sets it down with a chink. I watch his Adam's apple bobbing up and down, up and down, two gulps total. He wipes his mouth with the back of his hand then taps my knee. "Hold this will ya?" Stan hunches over and springs to his feet like a cat. He's squatting with his hands on the ledge and butt in the air.

Phoebe says, "Stop, you're not funny."

He says, "Relax, hon." With a great push of the forearms, Stan pops to his feet and stands upright. His arms point straight out like airplane wings. Phoebe screams when he wobbles cliff side. With one foot in front of the other, he walks the length of the wall like a tightrope walker.

Phoebe says, "If you love me, you'll cut it out."

Stan says, "Love's not like that, hon. Remember, everyone's gotta live their own life."

"But doesn't loving someone mean protecting them and keeping them from making mistakes?" Her voice is getting higher.

Stan says, "But everyone's gotta find their own way."

I say, "Exactly, isn't love about freedom? Loving someone unconditionally? Loving them despite their mistakes?"

Phoebe says, "You two are nuts! Finding your own way? And freedom?" Her voice is insistent now, sharp. I look over but Phoebe won't look at us. Her shoulders are slumped and she keeps her eyes straight ahead looking out at the prison and city lights.

She says, "I don't feel good Dad. Can we go home?"

"The fireworks will start up soon," he says.

"Please."

"What's wrong?" he asks.

"I have a headache."

"I'd hate to go when we just got here," he says.

She says, "If Kristen weren't feeling good we would have been in that car yesterday."

And instantly, Stan jumps down. He holds her chin in his hand and says, "Come on, don't do that. You're my number one lady. You know I love you." They walk off arm in arm to go look for aspirin. I can't think of the last time my father and I even touched.

Stan's wine bottle is wedged between my thighs. When I lift it, it's heavier than I'd imagined. I put the spout to my nose. It smells bad. The first sip warms my throat. The taste is unclear. First it's sour, and then it's bitter, then it has a little sweet after-taste. I try again and I take a bigger drink this time. It's easier when you just gulp it. It makes my head hot. It makes my skull soften, my neck looser. I drink more.

In front of me, the view is both so grand and so small all at once. Sometimes I think it's the smallness that scares me. That I will suffocate beneath the plastic. But then the bigness scares me too. Look at all those stars and seas, the lights that go on endlessly, red and white ribbons of traffic speeding by, everyone going somewhere and wanting something. Even the Dobermans look mean.

The scholarship deadline is three days away. Beneath my bed, I have my manila envelope stuffed with my poems, transcripts, letters of recommendation, a self-addressed stamped envelope. I'm just waiting on Stan now. He's been saying that he's almost done with the song. He says, "With poet-songwriter on your application, you're a shoe-in."

I kick my heels against the wall and watch the sediment as it crumbles. When I lean forward the rush of it is freeing. I hang off the edge, facedown. I want to see how far I can go before I feel like falling. I sip more wine. It's delicious. I smile back at the night seduced by those winking lights.

I think I see a deer running, a pair of wet shining eyes behind a bush. I lean farther out. The wine falls from my lap. The bottle clinks against rocks as it rolls down the mountain.

Back at the car Phoebe is sitting on the rear bumper with her arms folded to her chest. She's tapping her foot furiously and looking away from Stan. He's in the driver's seat. His head is on the steering wheel. His hand is in a fist on the dash. I see him turning the key but the car won't start.

Phoebe says, "The battery's dead. Dad shouldn't have left the music on."

"Does your dad have jumpers?"

Stan screams, "Damn it."

Phoebe says, "What do you think?"

"I guess they wouldn't have helped even if he did though right?" We're up on the peak of Mt. Tamalpais and Stan took side streets and illegal fire trails and nobody is around at all. The entire predicament makes me bust up. I can't stop laughing. I can barely stand it. I'm rolling on the pavement.

Stan stands over me. "If your parents knew, kiddo," he says and shakes his head. But then he turns his attention to the car. "Let's try and jump start it." Stan says that he'll push, Phoebe'll drive, and I'm in the passenger seat. The idea is that at the first turn off, Phoebe will pull in. Stan's going to walk down the hill and meet us there.

She's behind the wheel and freaking out.

"I'll do it," I say, "I want to drive!"

They say, "Yeah right!"

Stan says, "Now, when I say so, let go of the clutch. That's all you've gotta do." He's out of breath as he pushes the car along.

"I don't know," she says. "I just don't know."

Stan insists she'll be fine. He says, "I have all my faith in you, honey."

The engine fires up and we cheer. The wheels skirt the edge of the road. We scream at the top of our lungs. We're careening down the hill and then the fireworks start. Beautiful blossoms burst everywhere. We are up so high we see five shows: the one in Mill Valley and Richmond, Oakland and San Francisco, San Rafael too. There are pinwheels and starbursts and sparklers and rockets. Everything is in flight. Umbrellas of red and purple rain down blues and greens. I put my face to the sky. The heavens are near and the world lies before us, that's what Stan always says. It is warm. It smells like a bakery. The fireworks look like cupcake sprinkles and my mouth is open wide.

TAPS

Kim Le hovered with her ear to the bathroom door, listened to the sounds of bristles scraping against teeth, water swishing in his mouth, the urgency of piss splattering against the toilet bowl. Her hands in a funnel, she heard the squeak of the paper roll every three-quarter turn, the rumbling of pipes as he turned on the faucet, the rush of water when he cranked up the tap. Her cheek against the wall, she heard the swiping of a hand beneath the spout and then the hollowed clicking of fingernails against stainless steel. Together, they waited for the water to warm. Kim knew her husband Duc was an impatient man. She wondered if their roles were reversed, had she been the one locked up, whether he would have waited for her.

Pressing her weight against the grain of wood, she heard the tap-tap-tapping furious against the faucet. She pictured his trigger finger and wondered if it sometimes itched for the rattle of a machine gun. Wondered what he had suffered at the hands of his captors. Wanted to ask him if he had ever killed a man. And then she'd look at his hands and wonder what they were capable of. Since his arrival from Vietnam, she'd catch herself studying them, the veined brown muscles, nails cut to flesh, the thick blunt fingers, buttoning up a shirt, buttering bread, clenched into the tight fists of sleep. After two nights in the same bed his hands had yet to touch her.

After a decade of waiting, telling herself Duc was the love of her life, thinking if not for herself for the kids, praying that once he got here everything would be better, after ten long years, her husband had finally arrived, and Kim was living with a stranger.

Duc had been locked up as a prisoner of war. He'd been in the central highlands. She expected it to change a man. But she didn't expect what she got.

Kim readied herself to sharpen her ears, train her eyes. On the other side, he switched on the overhead fan. She pressed her ear even harder against the door. The whirring blades drowned out his movements. Outside the traffic horns blared. She shrugged her shoulders then shuffled away in her slippers.

At the kitchen sink washing plates, she cursed the fan, its camouflage effect, its ability to snuff out any bridge between how he could go from flossing teeth to tearing down her sunflowered shower curtain. How he could go from relieving himself to then slamming the toilet lid with such hatred she'd find it fractured in two. How he could go from brewing ginger tea to the sobbing cries she now heard slipping through the static murmur of the vents.

At the airport, she saw he was darker from the sun. He was skinnier from the lack of food. But mostly, he looked the same, walking through the terminal gate, tall and handsome, carrying all his possession in that one military green duffel bag. She'd wished then that she hadn't sent Marcel and Sophia to summer camp. Now though, she exhaled relieved.

Kim and Duc had written letters throughout the years. She thought it odd now that she hadn't asked more questions, harder questions. But truth was she welcomed the love letters. When the transparent sheets arrived from Vietnam, she got to trade in the exhaustion of life as a single mother in a foreign country for the easy past. Duc wrote about how he had once pursued her. He wrote about their mating games and rituals: Friday night movies, Saturday night durian shakes, Sunday morning coffee.

After an hour in the bathroom, Duc returned to the kitchen. He stood stiff, composed, a soldier's soldier, the officer that he'd once been. Both his upper and lower eyelids were swollen. He held his chin up though his eyes stayed downcast. He tried to shake off her gaze in a spastic jerk the way a dog might try to shake off water or dislodge a flea. He squeezed lemon into his now cold tea and then asked for honey.

She offered to brew him a new cup. But he said, "Do you have any or not?" He drummed the spoon on the lip of the cup.

"It's really no problem," she said. The silver spoon clinked against the counter. The lemon wedge dropped in the trash with a thump. The lid clapped shut.

From prison he would write, "You are my heart." "I'm staying alive for you and the kids alone." "When we are together again we will..." and they were always glorious dreams.

Kim leaned back against the sink's edge and watched his long stubborn back leaving the kitchen. She wanted to let him sulk, be a baby, what did she care? But she couldn't. She stopped him and said, "Here." She opened the cupboard door. "Help yourself. This is where I keep all the spices and condiments. This is now your home too." She placed the little plastic bear with the red tipped hat on the counter.

Duc picked up the bottle and rubbed the tips of his fingers together. She could hear its squish. He squeezed the rounded belly and when the bear's hat plopped off, honey oozed out on the counter. He cursed. Kim reached to wipe it with a sponge. But Duc swiped up the honey with his finger, placed his finger in his mouth, and sucked it. She stood paralyzed, watching. The wet sponge dripped on her toes. He freed his mouth and bared his teeth to her. He said, "You don't keep house the way you used to." He looked at her feet. "The floor is wet." She returned to the dishes. "Your back is wet too. Maybe you shouldn't fill the sink so high." Under his breath he said, "You've turned American."

She asked, "How?" But when she turned around he was already gone. He used to call her his honeybee, give her bouquets and have her suck the stems, every single flower chosen for the sweetness of its nectar.

In the living room, Duc changed the channels incessantly. Images flickered by of human bodies loving or abusing each other. He stared ahead with the television set on mute. All the while his thumb beat on the buttons, click, click, clicking.

She said, "I guess it's difficult finding anything worth watching." She leaned on the sofa and dried her shriveled hands on a dishtowel. Duc said nothing. He butted the plastic remote against the cushions of the arm rest. It made a dull thudding sound like boots stomping through mud.

"Hey there." She flicked his shoulder with the towel. He jumped and snatched it. He clutched the towel in his hand. They held on to opposite ends of the cloth. She thought of it as a playful gesture until she noticed that his lips had curled into what resembled a snarl. "Sorry," she said. He flung his end at her and released it.

Kim turned away so quick it made her dizzy. She steadied herself against the bureau's edge to catch her breath. The room was silent but for the staccato of Duc's nervous tapping. The apartment didn't feel the same without the racket of the kids horsing around and their bubbling jabber. Sophia and Marcel wouldn't have wanted to see their parents like this, she knew, and so she straightened up. She remembered her promise to them. She pulled a tape player out of the bureau drawer. She turned to him. "The kids made something for you. Do you want to see it? Or, actually, listen to it?"

The tape player was black and chrome and she laid it flat in the center of the coffee table. She pushed play and took a seat beside Duc on the sofa. They waited for the tape to start. Kim closed her eyes listening to the buzzing static. It hissed like a person's last breath until the clapping began and her daughter's voice lifted above the applause. She said, "Sophia was the lead in her school musical. It was called Annie. She had to wear a curly red wig." The singing began and Kim happily sank back into the cushions.

Duc edged forward in his seat. He clasped his hands together and dropped his head over the device. Sophia's voice was a brittle tinkle. It tip-toed along with timid steps. Kim saw Duc smile. He gulped and she could see him trying to decide what to say. Kim stopped the tape. "All the other parents have home movie recorders. But this was all I could afford. I thought hearing it would be better than nothing." She pressed play again. Kim had been pregnant with Sophia when he went to war. He had yet to meet his ten-year-old daughter.

From the machine, Sophia's soprano voice grew bolder and clearer. When she neared the climax, her lungs were thunderous. They pounded out the last *tomorrows* with the force of a hurricane. Kim remembered sitting in the school gym staring up at Sophia's little body on that makeshift stage in complete wonder, chills running up her spine. She saw that it had the same effect on Duc. His jaw quivered. He cleared his throat and said, "She inherited your voice."

"She might have inherited my ear." Kim paused to think a moment. "But no, that voice, it's an angel's voice. I have nothing to do with it." She wondered if he remembered the lullabies she'd sing to him when he couldn't sleep nights, the circles she'd draw on his back.

Next on the tape recorder was Marcel saying a few words to his dad in Vietnamese. *I'm glad you're here and now you can come to my baseball games*, he said.

Duc said, "Baseball?" He dropped three sugar cubes into his cup and then stirred cream into his tea.

Kim pointed to a photo displayed on the wall. "There he is in uniform with his team. He's obsessed. He thinks he'll go professional. You've got to remind him to stick with his books."

Duc said, "He looks like me." He said it smiling. And it was true. Kim could see it in the expanse between their eyes and mouth, the high cheekbones, the almost pretty feminine ears.

Marcel proceeded to do a beat-box thing with his mouth into the tape recorder. It sounded like warbled spitting, accompanied by tongue clicking, and heavy slobbering. He tried to imitate his new favorite band, a rap group called Run DMC that his cousins from San Jose had introduced him to. Kim didn't mind the musical influence although she hadn't liked the rest that she saw. The last time they visited, her nephews Frank and Dean were dressed like little thugs with oversized jeans and fake gold jewelry. She even noticed three burn marks in the shape of a triangle on Frank's upper forearm. She had grabbed his arm and asked, "Does your Dad know about this?"

Frank said, "How do you know he didn't do it himself," and pulled down his sleeve. He was only fifteen and she already saw him hunting for trouble. She feared Marcel taking such a turn and was grateful Duc had arrived just in time for the onset of those tough teen years.

Duc asked, "Is the boy burping in there?"

Kim laughed, "No, he just wanted to have a talent for you."

Noonday sunlight filled the room and warmth fell into their laps. Kim planned on taking Duc shopping later, new clothes, a new start. She walked to the window and leaned against the ledge. From her third floor vantage point she could see the vibrant green blades of grass beckoning from Delores Park and thought perhaps they could have a picnic later. She imagined delectable treats spread out on a blanket beneath the shade of the jacaranda tree. Her head would rest on his lap, he would stroke her hair like he used to, and the bloom of courtship would envelope them again.

She said, "The kids are excited to meet you. Especially Marcel, he missed you bad. He wants you to see what a man he's become." She returned to sit beside him on the couch. Duc nodded. Kim hesitated to say it because it wasn't customary for a woman to talk so boldly. But after ten years, she had to say it. "I've missed you too Duc. I've dreamed about this day." In her excitement she grabbed for his hand. He startled and pulled back. A neighbor slammed a door. The framed photos hanging on the wall vibrated momentarily and shifted in place. Duc flinched and blinked. Several minutes passed before he looked at her again.

Kim hauled out the heavy photo album after this. She wanted the old photos to stir up the old memories. Unfortunately, except for the photos of their children, Duc remained dazed and vacant-eyed. She would be pointing at someone, telling him who was living, and who was dead, or even worse divorced, and then she'd look up to find him staring out the window. Even the photos of their honeymoon in Da Lat seemed to bore him.

The black birch that leaned past the apartment ticked against the glass. The branch occasionally swiped the pane with the whoosh of the wind. The leaves jingled like chimes until they smooshed up flat against the window, covering the sun, darkening the room, throwing shadows over his face.

"This must be too much," she said. She gave him a stack of letters tied in red string. "Here, you can read about everyone at your own leisure." They were letters from the men he once commanded. The postmarks were from Berlin, and Sydney, Paris, and Cape Town, though most of course came from Santa Ana, California otherwise known as America's Little Sàigòn. Duc took the bundle and wedged it behind a cushion.

She said, "You know I'm your wife. You know we can talk about anything, right?"

"Of course, you're a good talker," he said. He looked down and scratched at his elbow. The back and forth of his fingernail made a starchy sound. She watched dried flakes of skin rain on the armrest. It reminded her of the scratch-off lottery tickets she stopped buying the day Duc arrived.

When she asked him, "How did you get out? Do you want to tell me what it was like?" He punched at the cushion on his lap. Then she tried with small talk. Did you get to read much? Didn't you once say there was a garden? Did the food get better? What did the labor involve? And then she asked something although she couldn't quite remember what. She remembered that the wind had picked up causing the branch outside to bang against the window. It slammed so hard she feared the window breaking. When the window didn't break, she thought it might be too windy for a picnic after all. Kim forgot what she had said to him though it must have been the wrong thing to say. Because the next thing she knew, he'd put both feet on the coffee table and kicked the whole thing over. The tea, cream, sugar, cups and saucers all went crashing down. The table legs stuck straight in the air like a dead bug on its back.

Duc holed up in the bedroom. Kim dialed immigration services. They transferred her to a counseling hotline. Her hands were still shaking while she sat on hold. The counselor said it was common. Duc was shell shocked, post traumatic stress disorder they called it. She could make an appointment for two weeks time. Until then, said the voice on the other end of the line, "Be patient. Ten years is sure to change a man."

Kim hung up the receiver. She decided to clean the apartment. She wanted to be more like a traditional wife. She figured that was what he meant when he had said that she was "American," earlier. Or did he mean that she shouldn't have questioned him? That she was too independent? Was that what it meant to be American? Or had he been brain washed by the Viet Cong? Did he mean that she now represented the enemy? Is this why he wouldn't touch her?

She picked up the table, mopped the floors, wiped down the doors, swiped and shined. She avoided the garbage disposal, the vacuum, anything loud. In the bedroom, she gathered her clothes. Laundry was safe. It was downstairs in the building's basement. Duc was lying down flipping through a magazine. She sat down beside him on the edge of the bed. "I have some old Vietnamese novels if you'd like to read." She pulled out the bedside drawer. The letters he'd written her were in there too. They were carefully preserved and wrapped in ribbon. "That's all of them," she said. "You were quite a romantic from jail."

"That's because I was being tortured."

"Very funny," she said. She handed him her favorite letter. "In this one, you write about how nervous you were to ask my father for my hand." Duc began reading it. Kim went about gathering the rest of her whites. She recited by heart, "I nicked myself shaving, stubbed my toe, and forgot my keys in the refrigerator. I'd lost my mind and had already given away my heart." She heard his laugh for the first time in ten years. It was the happiest she'd been in days.

Inside the closet, Kim saw his military duffle bag. She figured he at least had underwear to wash. She had only unzipped it when he bolted to her side. He screamed, "What the hell you think you're doing? Huh?" and tore the bag away.

"I just thought I could wash your clothes for you." She stammered over her words.

"What are you looking for? What do you want? Who told you to do this?"

"I used to wash your clothes for you," she said.

"I don't have anything," he said. "Keep out of my shit."

He crumpled the letter in the fury of his fist. She bit down so she wouldn't cry. She fought off the sinking suspicion that he was hiding something from her. She feared that perhaps he had another woman.

That night Kim wore her brand new silk pajamas to bed. She wanted him to be hers again. She thought back to their lovemaking in the rain beneath a canopy of pines on their honeymoon. She wanted him to know how much she loved him. But he didn't reach for her the way she thought a man would naturally reach for his wife. She lay on her side of the bed. He lay on his.

Duc was the only man Kim had ever been with. She thought about that fact while she stared sleepless into the dark. Before he came she had imagined them making love and then staying up until daylight confessing all the things that had happened in the years apart. The girls she worked with at Lee's Nails told her to take a week off work. "Take a break from doing other people's nails and get *your* nails done girlfriend!" They said, "Get dolled up." "Send the kids to camp." "Make the apartment the dream haven that man's been fantasizing about while stuck in a roach infested cellar." She saved up and followed each exacting detail because her friends said it would be like a second honeymoon.

When Kim thought about her wedding night, she found her

fingers wandering to her breasts. She always relied on the same images, the way his hand had looked splayed on her belly, his set jaw, the sound of his breath.

Outside their apartment, the bus squawked to a stop. Beside her, Duc began making sounds, moaning. He straddled her and she could feel his erection on her leg. She liked the familiar weight of him. Her body opened and warmed to his touch. Kim's hands were still under her shirt. She sighed in sync with his movement. But in the next moment, Duc began kicking violently. She tried to free her hands to wake him. But before she got a chance, he'd covered her mouth airtight until she could barely breathe. With his other hand, he clenched her throat and she tried to push him off but couldn't. She tried to scream but her voice was muffled. The harder she tried, the less breath she had especially with his weight on top of her. And then with the hand that had been on her mouth, he shoved her head into the pillow. He pulled her hair, found her ear, yanked it. She finally managed to scream, *"Ba! Ba!"* He pressed his fingers into the hinge of her jaw. He looked at her as if he'd never seen her before or just now recognized her for the first time. He kept blinking before finally releasing her.

Kim jumped out of bed. "Who are you? What have you done with my husband? I want my husband back!" She switched on the lamp and saw Duc curled in a ball on the far corner of the bed. His back was heaving, he was crying so hard he was choking. She wanted to hit him, kick him. But when she turned and saw herself in the mirror, a breast hanging out, hair a nest, the veins of rage on her temple, she fell to the ground. She pounded the carpet until her hands were sore. She kicked until both feet ached. She pulled her hair and scratched her arms, this stupid body she despised. Duc got up and she thought he was coming to her at last. But instead she watched his legs running right past her into the bathroom where he retched.

The buzz of light from the streetlamp shined through the open bathroom window. Duc was on the tile. He was on all fours with his forehead against the rim of the toilet. He had taken his shirt off to clean up the vomit. And then for the first time, she saw them. The scars like mountain ranges, crumbling down his back. His hand reached for them. He traced the contours down the length of his spine. He caressed them. His shoulders rounded, tensed, and then he began to moan. Duc curled his back and then rubbed the scars against the toilet bowl the way a cat nudges against a couch. He groaned and whimpered and then he let out a guttural grated sigh. She could not tell if he was pleasuring himself or if he was in pain, but from the edge of the hallway, listening, she knew he wasn't well.

Kim returned to the bedroom to find Duc a clean shirt to wear. She thought about giving him one of her shirts but feared insulting him with a lady's blouse. She went into the closet and reached for his duffle bag. Inside, she found his possessions including a Zippo lighter, a box of cigarettes, and a few pairs of underwear. At the very bottom, Kim was surprised to find a photo of herself. It was tattered and water-stained. It was the one that Bao, her brother's best friend had taken those many years ago. It showed her in repose beneath the shade of a lemon blossom with her youthful belly peeking out. Her eyes looked directly into the camera with a striking confidence but her small shaky smile betrayed her. She had liked that the photo captured her honestly and had given it to Duc at their last good-bye.

Kim returned the photo and was reaching for his shirt when her nail snagged on a plastic baggie. In the dim light, she couldn't make out what was in it. When Kim opened the bag it had a peculiar smell. She went to the bed, turned on the bedside lamp, and dumped out the contents. There were six of them. They looked like dried apricots shriveled and sliced thin. They were an earthen color perhaps gone bad from having been kept too long. The brown hues ranged from a purple brown to shades of dirt brown and pinkish brown. They were different sizes some bigger than others, distinct in shape, with a perfect smoothness on the curved side, and an abrupt jaggedness on the other. Although they had a brittle appearance, when she picked one up she found it had a rubbery texture. Kim held it up to the lamp. Under the brightness of the bulb there were tiny microscopic hairs on the outer ridge like peach fuzz. After a moment, Kim realized it was a human ear.

She recoiled and dropped it. She'd heard of this sort of thing before. People gossiped about Vietnam vets who'd gone crazy, returning with decapitated fingers, severed toes, a necklace of ears. Now before her, six of them were scattered on her bedspread.

She wondered whose they were. She pictured them attached to different heads. One of the ears was so shredded it looked like a scrrated knife had been used. One of them had a marking that looked like it had been a mole. Another one was peculiar because it was so concave. She imagined a man with ears like soup bowls having gone through adolescence a self conscious youth.

She wondered why her husband would keep these ears? Were these the ears of his captors, the prison guards, the torturers? Were they the ears from a memorable battle? Tokens that he'd hidden away, buried in a jail cell all of these years? Could they have meant this much to him?

There was an ear tucked beneath her pillow. It was so small she'd almost missed it. It had a short round earlobe. It looked delicate. There were seven in all then. This last one must have belonged to a child. She thought of Sophia and Marcel. She thought about Duc's hands. Outside her apartment window, a dog began howling. The dog homed in on her third floor window barking fiercely as if he had sniffed them out.

Kim looked around her bedroom. The objects looked familiar—the bookshelf, the framed photos, the hanging ivy, the potted plant, the ticking clock. Everything was the same but nothing was as it was. The woman who had inhabited this room, it was clear she was gone too.

Out in the hallway, the night light cast shadows over her feet. The carpet was matted. The heater hummed. The clock chimed. She paused before entering the bathroom. It was dark and muddled inside. With her palms flat against the walls, she braced herself like a blind person and felt her way to the sink.

She turned on the water. She washed her hands, scrubbed them hard, rubbed them until they were raw. She turned the tap on hotter. She splashed herself with scolding water. She wanted to melt. She let it drip down her face, down her throat, down her chest. Let it soak the lapel of her new silk shirt. She dropped her head until it almost hit the faucet. In its shiny reflection she saw a dimmed image of her face in pieces.

Down at her feet he shivered in a ball. She could hear his teeth chattering. The voice muttered louder. He rocked back and forth. His head beat against the toilet rim each time. Tap. Tap. Tap. Like the torture of a leaky faucet she thought. Tap. Tap. Tap. She turned it on full force.

THEY WERE DANGEROUS

Elle was older but Sophia had bigger breasts. Elle knew Sophia pretended not to like the attention they drew but always wore white t-shirts without a bra. She had a habit of talking with her hands folded together on top of her head. It caused her heavy breasts to lift even higher. They looked like nuclear missiles launching into flight. They were dangerous and Sophia knew it.

Everywhere they went people started saying, "Here comes double trouble." Although they had hung out together all of their lives, that year they suddenly started to receive attention from older men. They were too young to go to bars so they went to cafes instead. Men bought them sweet syrupy coffee drinks and made eyes at them over caramel lattes or steaming mocha biancas. The men said things like, "You're lucky I'm not your age," with a wink like an exclamation mark.

These men. They had a thing for women who looked like each other. Elle and Sophia weren't twins, but they were cousins. This was good enough. They also had a thing for Asian girls, these guys. Whether they were at the mall or a coffee shop, some guy would have to approach with a one-liner in Japanese, or Chinese, or Thai. The men would say, "You're so exotic, where are you from?" When the girls said Vietnam, the guys would say that they had fought there, or their uncles had, or mention Agent Orange. Or like today, just a moment ago, a software engineer in khaki pants said something dorky about Rambo.

Elle had whispered to Sophia, "The only Rambo for me is Speed. He can ram me anytime." Speed's real name was Anthony Spee but everyone including the high school principal called him Speed because he ran track and always placed gold. They had AP Bio together.

Sophia said, "Speed's a pretty boy. Why can't you like someone more edgy?"

"Isn't he? He's beautiful." Elle drew out the –ful so it was smoky and scorched. It matched how Speed looked at her, a gaze like a slow burn. He was so hot the tips of his eyelashes were singed the color of burnt gold as if he emanated heat from the inside out.

Above them, the sky was a brilliant blue and the midday sun bleached out the buildings. They sat beneath the white umbrella of a sidewalk café called The Steps of Rome. Their favorite Saturday pastime was to sit in North Beach and watch traffic go by while making occasional faces at hapless tourists in cable cars. "Check him out," said Sophia. A guy on a black and chrome vintage motorcycle roared up to the curb.

The motorcycle man took off his helmet to reveal a short buzz cut. Although he had on a young outfit, tight jeans and a Sex Pistols t-shirt, he had salt and pepper sprinkled in his side burns. Elle was wearing her Daisy Dukes and he checked out her legs. They were still tanned from canoeing down the Russian River last weekend. It was deflating when just as quickly his focus shifted to Sophia's white t-shirt. After he ordered his coffee, he returned to sit at the table beside them. He pulled out his chair causing the legs to make an awful grating sound. He probably did it on purpose because the second they turned, he took the opportunity to ask, "So you go to State?"

He was lanky and tall. When he tried to cross his legs, he bumped into the underside of the table. It caused the coffee to splatter over the lip of his mug.

His ears reddened, and for a second Elle felt sorry for him. She said, "No, we're still in high school. She's a freshman. I'm a junior."

He said, "Too bad, you're not even legal yet." Then he turned to Sophia and said, "You're so exotic, you remind me of my snake."

Elle couldn't believe that she was sucker enough to be sympathetic a minute ago. She thought it was a boring line because the word exotic was so played out. Six months ago, a rich white lady had approached her and said the exact same thing. "You're so exotic." The woman had reached for Elle's chin and cupped it. Elle remembered her hand smelling of cigarettes and bruised gardenias. She had declared, "Cupid lips and a face like a perfect little China doll!" Elle felt special because a rich woman had picked her out to compliment. Then the husband with the big hands and tiny espressos turned to his wife and said, "Wouldn't her skin look lovely in the white interior of our white Rolls Royce?" When Elle had wanted to leave the café early that day, Sophia hadn't understood.

"It's not like it's a put down," said Sophia. It was hard for Elle to explain that it didn't make her feel ugly but rather like she didn't even exist.

The motorcycle guy was now going on about how sexy and different Sophia was and she seemed to like it. The guy said, "Hold on," and returned to his bike. He was digging around in the hatch, and from out of nowhere he lifted a boa constrictor into the air. It was brown and gray and coiled itself up and around his hairless arm. He asked, "Do you want to touch it?"

Elle kicked Sophia beneath the table and said, "He might be like the guy from the River."

Sophia laughed but went to him anyway.

Last weekend, Elle's soccer team had organized a canoe trip fundraiser. Elle and Sophia were in a canoe together when a nude man with a jiggling gut chased them in the shallow end and screamed, "I'm gonna gitcha good, you nasty little girl." He had his thing in his hand and he jerked it back and forth like he was loading ammunition. Elle wondered which of the two he intended to "git."

It gave Elle the creeps but Sophia still petted the thing. At first she hesitated and only dabbed it with her finger. She did it ever so gently the way the woman behind the cosmetics counter had taught them how to apply eye cream without tugging at your skin. The motorcycle guy urged Sophia on. He said, "Go on. Don't be shy." Next thing she knew, Sophia was full on stroking the thing and giggling with delight.

In bed at Sophia's house that night, Sophia said, "Even though the snake looked like it would be slippery and moist, it was actually dry." She hissed the word "moist" because she knew Elle thought the word sounded perverted.

Elle said, "Yuck, shut up!"

Elle liked spending the night at her cousin's because Sophia's mom, Aunt Kim, was never home. They could do whatever they wanted.

The Communists had locked up Sophia's dad before she was even born. There was a time when he was finally going to get released. In the months before his arrival, Aunt Kim was happier than Elle had ever seen her. Her aunt's entire comportment was different. Her back seemed straighter. She was chipper. She reminded Elle of a hummingbird buzzing about to beautify herself and her home for his arrival. But in the end he never made it. Aunt Kim told us, "There was some bureaucratic mistake. They say he can't come to America. Ever."

Aunt Kim was younger than Elle's mom but she looked older. Elle suspected the lines on her aunt's face were etched in to match the depths of her despair. After the disappointment with Uncle Duc, she started going out late night and gambling all the time.

Aunt Kim said she slaved away working two jobs to raise two kids on her own. In truth, Marcel was barely around. He was pitcher on the varsity baseball team and was practically being raised by the coach. They were grooming him to take the team to State and to get an athletic scholarship to college. If Marcel wasn't staying over at the coach's or traveling with the team, he was eating over and staying the night at his girlfriend's house. Everyone knew his curveball was his ticket out and no one got in the way. Aunt Kim barely made enough to feed a growing sixteen-year-old boy. Her money went to paying off men who had long pinky nails, drove low rider cars with shiny rims, and spoke bad English.

Aunt Kim found solace in being able to say, "Thank God Marcel plays ball. He could have ended up like Frankie."

Elle used to secretly think Frank was the cutest of her boy cousins until he showed up at a family reunion with a chopped-off pinky finger. The deformity freaked her out. She found out from little Sammie, who was still young enough to want to be good, that it marked his promotion to Lieutenant in the Asian Boyz. On the car ride home, her mom said to her dad, "How did Lam let his boy get so out of control."

It was scary how they had all started off in the same house at 22nd Ave. and now everyone was spinning off in wildly different directions. Nobody realized exactly how out of control Uncle Lam's house was until he was found shot through the back of the head inside the driver's seat of his car. At first the cops thought it was just a robbery gone bad. Uncle Lam's wallet, his watch, and the rims of his brand new Acura were stolen. But later, it was linked to Frank's gang-banging. And in the end, they came up with evidence to say it was an ordered hit, likely ordered by Frank himself.

The court papers said that when the detectives showed up at the house to tell Aunt Trang about her husband's murder, she answered the door with a black eye. They also noted the deep bruises around her wrists. Frank was quoted in the investigation report as saying, "I didn't do it but I'm not sorry to see him gone." For the time being, he was being held at the Main Jail Complex in downtown San Jose until he was sentenced. Aunt Trang kept calling Elle's mom to cry and say over and over, "It's my fault." Elle's mom never spoke about it, no matter how much Elle would beg her. In her mom's point of view, it was a disgrace to the family and a tragedy too awful to speak of. Talking about it meant admitting the truth not just about Frank but Uncle Lam too. What had he done to drive his son to this edge?

Tonight, Aunt Kim was out gambling again. In bed, Elle's stomach grumbled and Sophia turned to say, "What was that?" They had only had two bowls of cereal each for dinner. Elle kept secret these small details from her own mother who surely wouldn't approve and wouldn't let her stay the night if she knew.

It was one of those uncommonly warm spring nights in San Francisco. Sophia said, "It's so hot, I'll take off my shirt if you do." She wanted to show off her chi-chis every chance she got. Then she said, "What about our bottoms too?"

The window was wide open and in the far distance they could hear the steel wheels of the J Church grinding against the tracks. Sophia said, "That guy with the snake looked like he might have had a huge snake in his jeans too, don't you think?" She widened her eyes big when she said this and the whites of them glowed in the dark.

Elle said, "What do you know about that?" She whacked Sophia over the head with a pillow. Elle was older. If there was going to be an expert on that matter, she was supposed to be the one. And yet, they both knew that Sophia was more experienced. She had already let three guys go to second base with her. Two of them had grabbed for Sophia's breasts before they even kissed her.

Sophia threw the pillow back and sat up against the rattan headboard. She sighed, "I'm sorry, but I'm serious, he had on such tight jeans."

Even in the dark, Elle could make out that Sophia's breasts were so full, the bottom part rested on her upper ribs. Her nipples stood out erectwhen a cold chill suddenly pushed through the window.

When Elle first started noticing boys, her father took her aside to tell her about his courtship with her mom. "Do you know that it used to take me over six hours each way to go on a date with your mom? I had to get on a bus in Can Tho that then boarded two ferries to cross two different sections of the Mekong Delta. And once I got to the other side, I had to hire a cyclo driver to take me to your mom's house in this out of the way district of Sàigòn. When I finally arrived, we would sit in the living room drinking tea under the supervision of her parents." Yet he told the story with a smile on his face.

Maybe that's why Elle couldn't go anywhere past first base unless she thought the guy respected her. She also had to respect the guy. If she even kissed someone and later learned he was an idiot, it made her feel sick inside like she had been polluted. Elle wondered if it was different for Sophia because her dad wasn't around. There was nobody to tell her these old-fashioned love stories.

Sophia said, "Chile Relleno," and slid back under the covers. A draft settled in the space between their bodies. Elle curled up like a shrimp and pulled the blanket over her shoulder.

Elle made a shivering noise and said, "It's so cold it's *Chile con Carne*." This word-game was an ongoing joke they shared. She added, "It's so freezing, it's *Chili* Davis," for the Giants baseball player. They both cracked up.

Sophia asked, "Should we put our clothes back on?" She said it into the back of Elle's neck so close that her breath tickled. Her new breasts flattened into Elle's back. Elle wondered what it would be like to press her face into them, between them. They reminded her of fresh baked bread loaves, full and hearty. Elle ignored Sophia's question and hoped to fall asleep with them resting warm, soft, and safe behind her.

That spring, temperatures hit record highs with days that matched Sacramento and Fresno. Everyone wore less clothes. There was an electric buzz in the air. Elle's skin tingled beneath the sunlight. Her favorite dress was a backless fluorescent orange spandex tank dress. Sophia told her, "It forces everyone's line of vision to automatically drift down to your butt. That's your best asset, you've gotta work it." Sophia was younger but she had a knack for these things. She of course, knowing her best assets, relied on her usual outfit, the white t-shirt. Weekends were the best. They liked to get dolled up and see how much free stuff they could get.

Sunday morning before going to Speed's track meet, they decided to go to their favorite ice cream parlor. They liked the 1950s retro look of the place, with the vintage jukebox, and shiny stools, and the framed black and white photos of old Hollywood movie stars. They also liked the fact that the old man who owned it would often give them an extra scoop. He had a thick German accent and he said, "I know you like coffee. Just like a grown up!" He pinched Elle's cheek. "How about an extra scoop of that Rum Raisin?"

After he scooped out the extra scoop with his ham-like forearm, he pointed to his cheek and said, "I'm waiting...." Because she stood there and didn't give him a kiss, he shook his finger at her and said, "You are a smart girl. You Asians, you're clever."

His smudged white apron squeezed out from behind the counter to hand them each a cone. He had small thick hands and sausage fingers that he grazed her side with. He pretended it was an accident and Elle let him but she didn't smile. She knew nothing was free even if they told you it was free. Eventually, they'd always want something from you.

Sophia flashed a smile and said, "Yum, thanks! You're the best."

He caught Elle looking at the photos of the movie stars hanging behind the counter. "Someone once told me that a man is considered sexy when he is cool and distant like James Dean or Marlon Brando, you see." He turned his mouth upside down and rubbed his chin as if looking back on his own life and reflecting on everything he wasn't. "But for a woman it is different. She is considered sexy by men when she is nice and friendly." He smiled directly at Sophia as if to praise her friendliness, and to remind Elle that there was more she could do. Elle frowned but he continued on.

"She is considered sexy when she seems to be available to the entire public like Marilyn Monroe for instance," he pointed to a photo of Marilyn holding down her white dress. "Even when in fact she isn't!" He declared it like a victory and an accusation all at once. He turned to Elle and scowled at her, as if she was guilty of a crime she had not known she'd committed.

Outside, Elle asked Sophia, "Would you rather be smart or pretty?"

"Both."

"But someone's holding a gun to your head and you can only pick one."

Sophia didn't hesitate. "Pretty," she said. "Life is easier. Pretty is power." Sophia's tongue lapped up the Rum Raisin perched on her sugar cone. "C'mon give me a break. You think Speed's going to go for you because you're smart."

In Vietnam, Elle's mother had always been considered the pretty one. Her uncles told her, "Before she met your dad, she had suitors spiraling around the house. Your mother was the *Tin Sáng* Spring Queen. Some guys went as far as climbing the mango tree outside the courtyard just so they could get a look at her." Aunt Kim on the other hand was known for her sense of humor, her brain for science, the sweet richness of her egg noodle soup. It had been the same for Elle and Sophia all their lives too. Sophia had been nothing but the bratty baby. Suddenly she got these mounds and then she was instantly "mature." Elle hadn't cared much about being pretty before. She had always tried to be the smart one. Her love of books developed because she had been afraid of only being seen and not heard.

There were people like her friends' dads who were supposed to be one way but now acted differently than before. Both single and married ones started flirting with her. Her friend Pam Pure's dad got in the habit of calling her Elle-Belle, which she didn't mind once he told her it meant "beautiful" in French. A couple of weekends ago, Pam Pure's dad even told her a dirty joke at the soccer game. One minute, he had called her over by saying, "Come have a chat with me, kiddo," something innocent like that. And then suddenly, the conversation diverged into lowered voices and fidgety eyes. Afterward he said, "Elle, you've really got an old soul." It was confusing to figure it out.

More and more Elle questioned what people meant when they said, "You're pretty." Did they mean the particular formation of her face, or did they mean pretty like an exotic oriental rug that took a long time to weave, or did they meant slutty, like the Asian prostitutes inhabiting every single American war film? It was as if they never saw her at all. It was scary how things could change so quickly overnight. Like packing a suitcase and leaving your country behind forever.

As they waited for the bus in the Mission, men in low rider trucks blaring mariachi music hissed at them. The men in luxury cars did the opposite. These men seemed to fight with themselves not to look but sometimes just couldn't help it. There was a skateboarder they both thought was cute until he squeezed his crotch in offering as he sped away.

When they finally arrived at the track meet, Elle scanned the field for Speed's blonde head. He was in a relay event, hunched over waiting for the baton. On the sidelines, kids were running back and forth in either red or blue uniforms warming up.

Almost as soon as they entered, the school Narc spotted them and made a beeline in their direction. He had bright blue eyes that were bird-like in the way they darted about unblinking. They held your attention because the rest of his face was just dirty teeth and a goatee. Sophia waited for him and folded her hands on top of her head like a runway strip awaiting her jet's landing. Elle didn't like him. She left to find a seat in the stands.

Sophia probably felt indebted to him because he let them off the hook last month when he had caught them cutting class. They had been out by the tree line bordering the school and goofing around. They dared each other to pee behind one of the eucalyptus trees. When they finally decided to squeeze through the chain link fence that officially meant you were "off campus," somebody suddenly said, "Stop." A blanket of leaves carpeted the ground and they didn't even hear him approach. He could have been spying on them the entire time. They'd looked at each other freaked out. They said nothing until Sophia mouthed the word, "Shit." But it was also Sophia who had the nerve to turn it on, who'd turned around and said in a super sweet voice, "We're so sorry, *pretty please*, we promise not to do it again."

He said, "Come with me," and pulled out a set of keys from the front pocket of his baggy jeans. Elle had seen him lurking around before. He usually hung out by the lockers and often enough was checking out the freshman girls. He led them toward the parking lot and they followed him. It was the opposite direction from the principal's office but Elle would have done anything to avoid getting written up. When they reached his black Impala, he popped the trunk and offered them beers. Elle wasn't sure if it was a trick. She paused. Sophia on the other hand had jumped into the back seat looking utterly pleased. The Narc turned to Elle and said, "Riding shot gun?" He tried to look inviting but she could only see his sharp yellow incisor glinting in the sun.

Inside the car, Sophia leaned forward and whispered in Elle's ear, "I can't believe he didn't write us up." Sometimes, Sophia could be like a kid.

The Narc drove them off campus, up to a hillside where kids sometimes went to make out. It offered a view of the school and the city. They parked beneath an oak tree with a direct view of the school track. The Narc kept pitching the fallen oak balls against the trunk as if he was on a baseball mound. He said he almost made it pro. Then he made a noise by sucking air and spit through his molars. It was a sound filled with regret.

Elle and Sophia watched the girls from the P.E. class they had just cut running in circles below. The girls with bad BO panted behind the pack. Every now and then, one would knock over a hurdle and someone would fall. Everyone wore blue short shorts with a serial number on the right leg. A soft breeze tickled the oak leaves and they shimmered in the sunlight. In that moment, standing on the elevated ridge, Elle felt young and invincible. She took a swig from her beer and clicked cans with Sophia. Their bracelets jangled. She said to Sophia, "Isn't it cool to be a girl?"

But now, from the bleachers looking down on to the field, it bothered her the way the Narc stood over her cousin and talked to her breasts the entire time. He reminded her of a vulture, specifically, the white-headed vulture that she learned about in AP Bio. The white-headed ones arrived first and cautiously approached the carcass before tearing open the hide and allowing other types of vultures to feed. Elle wondered how old he was.

A group of boys from the other school walked by and eyed Sophia up and down with blunt lust. Elle shouted through the funnel of her cupped hands, "Sophia!" Her cousin turned to her, nodded, and then returned her attention to the Narc. She flipped her long black hair, put one hand on her hip, and jutted a knee toward him. Elle recognized Sophia's signature moves and thought it was wasted not only because he was old but because he was the Narc and he looked like a rodent.

In response, Elle pulled a book from her backpack. She knew Sophia hated it when she read in public. Sure enough, Sophia instantly marched up the stands to say, "You're tripping. Put that thing away." She insisted that, as one of the few "cool" Asians at their school, it was their responsibility to "fight the stereotype." Then she added, "Jeremy's pretty cool."

"Jeremy?"

"The Narc."

"You're calling the Narc by his name now?"

"Anyway, he offered to take us to Baker Beach if we want to cut Monday. He said it's supposed to be hot enough for us to wear our bathing suits and tan." Sophia shrugged to affect indifference although her eyes told a different story because they shined with glee. "I told him we're moving to LA after graduation because we love the beach. So he offered."

Looking at the other girls with their fresh faces and sporty clothes, Elle felt like a cheap offering in her tight spandex dress. But the hot orange dress worked. Before the meet was over, Speed raced by, tapped her shoulder, and as he jogged backward said, "Want to do something later?"

From a distance a girl in his pack of friends shot her a hard look. Elle recognized her as one of those girls with a name that matched her hair color like Amber, Ginger, or Ashley. Elle pulled down her dress and drew together the knobby knees she hated. Speed's head towered over the others. He winked at her when he thought no one was looking. It made all the difference. Sophia pinched her butt and said, "Ooohh, he wants you bad. Are you gonna do it later?"

Elle said, "Totally. Hard-core barely legal baby." They could joke about it because they had made a pact with each other to only do it at the same time. Elle was certain that it was years away anyway.

The girls rushed back to Elle's house so she could pack an overnight bag to spend the night at Sophia's again. When they got home, Elle's mom answered the door and said, "Good, you're right in time for dinner."

Elle told her mom that they weren't hungry and were just dropping by to get stuff for school tomorrow. Her mother replied, "Exactly, school tomorrow is precisely why you need to stay home tonight."

The girls followed her mom down the hallway and Elle pleaded to her mom's back, "Please, just tonight."

Her mom said, "What are you a vagabond now? Did I raise some sort of tramp?"

Her mom told them to go set the table. She added, "Your sister stayed home all weekend to help me around the house. We made an entire stock pot of *bò kho* yesterday."

Elle said, "Mom, I can't help it if Michelle doesn't have a life." Even though Michelle was close in age to Elle and Sophia, it was as if she was a galaxy away. Michelle was a little jock who lived for her softball team and didn't even like boys yet.

Sophia slapped Elle's shoulder. "I told you, we shouldn't have come here." She pretended that she was annoyed and was forced to stay. Yet during dinner, Sophia kept saying yum this and yummy that and said, "Wow, this is better than restaurant food." She helped herself to two servings of the shrimp salad and two servings of the shaking beef dish. Elle's mom was pleased to feed Sophia. She kept turning to her daughters to say, "Your cousin is such a healthy eater. You should be more like her."

After dinner in her bedroom, Elle said, "This sucks. Should I just call him? He's going to think I'm a flake. I can't believe my luck." She threw herself on the mattress with a thump. "Scoot over."

Sophia screamed, "Watch it!" She was sitting on Elle's bed painting her nails a color called Dragon Lady Red. She said, "Sneak out." Sophia pointed her chin toward the direction of the kitchen. "Sliding door," she said, "Tell him you'll be late. Your parents go to bed at like 10, right? So tell him you'll be there around 10:30 or 11. No biggie."

Sophia suggested it as if it was the most natural response

in the world though for Elle it was revolution. Elle was certain it was the perfect plan when Sophia was there. But after her cousin left, Elle second-guessed every little detail. What if someone broke into the house that night because she had to leave the sliding door unlocked? What if her parents called the cops because they thought she had been abducted? What if her parents caught her? But when she asked herself, what if this was her only chance with Speed and she blew it? Elle knew she had to go.

Despite the risk she took, her date with Speed only meant hanging out at the same track he ran circles around everyday. They were able to sneak in because Speed was team captain and the coach entrusted him with the gate key. They sat beneath the stadium lights and sipped from a forty of Mickey's he'd stolen from his dad. They passed it back and forth until the third time around he leaned in and licked her neck while she was still sipping from the bottle. She pulled away but he pulled her in and said, "You want to be my partner tomorrow?" They were dissecting frogs for AP Bio.

They kissed on the bleachers, and she thought about all those Saturdays when she had sat in these very seats and watched him from afar. Now she was so close in the nook of his neck, she learned that he smelled overwhelmingly of molasses and milk. He purred and stuck his tongue in her ear. "This is what you do to me," he said, and placed her hand over his pants.

It was the first time she had ever touched one. She pulled back when Speed tried to guide her hand beneath his jeans. He flinched at her reaction, but quickly shrugged it off. He continued to sip from the beer and then started kissing her again, and finally reached for her hand to guide it back down a second time. When she resisted again, he said, "What's up?" and cocked his chin back.

"Nothing. What's up with you?"

Speed chucked the beer bottle on to the field. He looked at her. "Cock tease," he said, "Slut." She watched the foam sputtering onto the Astroturf. He closed his fingers into a fist and punched the bleacher seats beneath them. He ran his fingers through his hair. Finally, he shoved his fists in his pockets and stomped down the bleachers. From the field he looked up at her and asked, "What the hell do you want from me?" Even from the distance she still saw his desire for her beneath his jeans. Speed walked away unspeaking.

Elle wanted to call Sophia and get a malted shake together. She wanted to calm her nerves and talk about what a dick he really was. She wanted to talk about how different boys were, how it was that they could both want you and hate you at the same time. She realized she was lucky he hadn't pushed her or hit her. Nobody was around. It made her realize late it was and how alone she felt.

She stood up and walked down the steps of the bleachers. Elle focused on the sound of gravel sloshing beneath her sneakers to keep her mind from racing when a low moan emitted from beneath the bleachers. She jumped, frightened. In the shadows, she saw a girl hunched over with her hands on her knees as if playing leap frog. Behind her was the Narc. He held on to the sides of her hips. The Narc looked up and stopped what he was doing. The girl turned and looked directly at Elle before quickly turning away.

Sophia wasn't at school the next day. When she showed up at Elle's doorstep after school, her hair was unruly, tousled, and salt-glazed. She smelled of the sea and her nose was red. She flopped onto Elle's bed and the first thing she said before "Hi" or "How are you?" was, "It was so much fun. You should have been there. Ashley did a beer bong and then got in the water without her top on. And Jeremy paid for everyone's beers."

"Why were you with Ashley?" Ashley was the leader of a clique of six girls called the six-pack. They were known for being fast and fine. They were popular, rich, and white. They were a year older than Elle, two years older than Sophia, and Sophia worshipped them.

Sophia said, "Jeremy's friends with the six-pack. I was waiting for you when they came by."

"Whatever. Thanks for waiting."

"You didn't even want to go, right?"

"Whatever."

"What's your problem?" Sophia popped up from the bed.

"I mean if you need to do it with the Narc to hang with the six-pack, it's your deal."

Sophia said, "What are you talking about? The Narc's disgusting. He looks like a rat. He always has mashed food stuck in his teeth. I'm insulted." Elle concentrated on the layer of sand Sophia had left behind on her white comforter.

She didn't believe Sophia but she didn't question her either. All she wanted was for them be on the same side again. "Sorry," she said. "I had the worst night ever last night." Elle broke down and cried. She told Sophia about her date with Speed.

Sophia said, "You're not missing out on much. Both Ashley and Lonnie said he sucks in bed." Sophia said it in a matter of fact way that made Elle feel uneasy. Elle continued to joke along although a couple of times she caught herself feeling like the last person to get the punch line of a joke. This had never happened with them before.

The next morning while walking to school, Elle found herself dragging behind to see if Sophia's gait had changed. Sophia wore her Bongo jeans and Elle noticed that her butt had not gotten any bigger but she did seem to walk a bit bow-legged. After school at Sophia's house, Elle checked the bathroom cabinets to see if her cousin had started using tampons. Before dinner, while Sophia was in the shower, Elle made the ultimate discovery and uncovered two condoms in Sophia's underwear drawer.

Elle held up a blue condom and said, "See I knew it was you!"

Sophia had just gotten out of the shower and only wore a white towel wrapped around her head. She said, "Excuse me?" and swerved her neck with such attitude that the towel flopped over.

"I knew you did it with him, so why deny it?"

Sophia pushed Elle aside. "I don't know what's wrong with you anymore. Let me get my underwear you tripper." Sophia snapped on her brand new Victoria Secret leopard print bra. "Don't you remember we hid them together? For when we decided that the time was right? One for me and one for you?"

Elle, remembering said, "Oh."

Sophia had her back to Elle and was trying to squeeze into some stretch jeans but Elle still heard her say under her breath, "I wish you trusted me." In the mirror of the sliding glass door, she saw Sophia rolling her eyes.

For the rest of the week, Elle and Sophia hung out less during school hours. Her cousin started hanging with the six-pack any chance she got. Elle and Sophia used to cut class only occasionally when one or the other was on her period and couldn't deal with changing clothes and running around for P.E. But now, Sophia turned it into a daily habit.

The following week, Sophia would come by during dinnertime, eat with Elle and her family, and then after dinner, they huddled together in Elle's bedroom so Sophia could recount her adventures. On Tuesday she said, "We hung out in Ashley's basement and everyone got high on hash and those little canisters you suck air from. Ashley's dad is a dentist." On Wednesday she said, "Oh my god, you'll never believe it. Ginger called her mom a bitch to her face when her mom caught us cutting after lunch." On Thursday she said, "Jessica's parents have a fully stocked bar with fancy crystal containers we poured hard liquor from." Hard liquor was a term Sophia had never used before. Elle remembered this detail as the defining moment when she knew Sophia had slipped away.

On Friday night Sophia said, "Half of the six pack have slept with Speed. They said, 'he wasn't all that.'" When Elle got pissed about it, Sophia said, "You're just jealous." Sophia had come by to get ready at Elle's. She was going to her first ever college keg party. One of the six-pack's older brothers was throwing it. Elle couldn't go. Her soccer team had an away tournament for the entire weekend. The bus was leaving at dawn.

Sophia wore a red lipstick that matched her Dragon Lady nail polish. She puckered her lips and said, "C'mon, please are you sure?" She had on one of those tank tops with a built in bra that looks like a negligee with white lace on the edges. One of the straps slipped from her shoulder and she left it dangling. She was scratching at an itch on her elbow when she said, "The college guys will be so much more mature! You're missing out." She oozed youth and sex appeal and a dangerous vulnerability that the other girls of the six-pack didn't possess. Even Elle could see that.

Elle said, "Be careful cuz."

At the soccer tournament in Pismo Beach, the fields were beautifully manicured, the crowds cheered with spirit, gulls cried out overhead, and their team won both their games. It was a good weekend to feel optimistic and hopeful. Pam Pure asked Elle, "Do you want to share a locker next year?" Pam knew about things like Ivy League schools and scholarships. Pam said, "They're such losers here, there's no way I'll end up stuck at State." Her eyes glazed over traveling to the faraway land of her successful future. When she snapped back she said, "You should come over and study for the SAT with me next weekend. My dad made flash cards. We go to TGIFs for potato skins and ranch if my practice scores are in the 90th percentile."

Her friends from the soccer crowd, girls like Pam were sensible. They did sports and ran for student government and cared about their future. Elle told herself she would rather hang with them than the six-pack anyway. The six-pack had rich dads who would pay for them even if they didn't get good jobs or didn't go to college. She pretended to forget about the bad dreams she'd had of Sophia stuck in a well and calling for help even though Elle could do nothing to help.

On Monday, Elle cut AP Bio to find her cousin. She knew Sophia would be in front of the 7-11 around the corner. The six-pack hung out there because they could bum cigarettes off of people and ask older men to buy them beers. Elle was relieved when Sophia called out to her. "Hey! What's up cuz?" and pulled her in with a hug.

Elle whispered in her ear, "If you can't beat'em, join'em right?"

The other girls were scheming about how to get alcohol. Elle decided they weren't so bad. They were no different than she and Sophia had been when they used to work it for free ice cream or a free latte. The stakes were just higher now.

Ashley said, "Here, want a drag?" Elle knew it was a sort of test. She watched the glow of the orange tip as it passed through the air toward her. She brought the lipstick-rimmed filter to her mouth and sucked. The inhale caught in her chest and she choked. Everyone laughed and Sophia patted her back.

Right when the head rush hit a big gray Buick sedan pulled into the lot. The girls hushed up. They assessed the man with thinning hair behind the wheel. He had on mirrored rimmed aviator glasses like the kind that cops wear. He sat and watched them and the girls said, "Yep, he's the one. He has that horny look." They were deciding whose turn it was to flirt with him to ask for the beer buy.

Jessica said, "I feel bloated today. Not me."

Ginger said, "Not for a guy who drives a Buick."

Ashley said, "I'm always the one."

Sophia said, "My cousin can."

Elle knew what she was getting into today and had prepared. Last night she had laid out her outfit: a blue jean mini skirt, a clingy pink cotton shirt, a push-up bra, and the whitest sneakers she owned. The girls coached her, "Smile and don't say much." They also unbuttoned the top three buttons of her top.

As she walked over to the car, she told herself to be brave. She looked down at her barely-there cleavage. It was true, Sophia had bigger breasts but still Elle was older and she had to be around to look after her cousin. As planned, when she was three feet away from his car, she accidentally dropped her change. She had to bend over in a certain manner and pick up each dime and nickel, one by one so that she felt a breeze between her thighs. After she had picked up each coin she stood with her hands tucked in her pockets and smiled at him shyly. She looked back at the girls who were sitting on the guardrail of the 7-11 pretending not to watch.

Elle pulled Sophia's signature move and ran her fingers through her hair and folded her hands on top of her head. When the man exited the car, he walked right up to her. Before he even removed his sunglasses, she blurted out, "Hi. Could you possibly buy me some beer?"

The man knitted his brows together. He took off his sunglasses and squinted into the sun and said, "Elle-Belle?"

It was Pam Pure's dad. His lips began moving as if trying to work out and weigh what he was going to say next. But no words came out. Elle looked back at the six-pack waiting anxiously. A few of the girls had gotten off the guardrail and now stood with their hands clasped upon their chests as if in prayer. Elle turned to Sophia who nodded at her and then blew a smoke ring into the air, a small tribute. Ashley was nodding her head too and repeatedly mouthed the same words, *Work-it, work-it.* And then Mr. Pure cleared his throat and before he could say anything, she ran.

Elle ran right past the school, past the track field, past the church, and the storefronts, and her favorite ice cream stand. She ran until she was out of breath and until her body hurt and until she was in such pain that she could no longer think. She wanted to stop thinking about how lame she must have looked and how stupid she was. Elle wanted to forget the image of Sophia's horrified expression and how she had covered her face with her hair in shame.

After the incident, the six-pack girls were icy and Sophia didn't come by after school any more. Sophia was with the six-pack so often that it was rumored they either they had to change their name (since now their were seven of them) or they were going to dump Jessica who had grown a little chubby.

At school, Speed told everyone she was "one of those uptight Asian chics." Elle even felt weird on the soccer team now. She was never sure if Mr. Pure had said anything to his daughter or anyone else. She became a self-imposed loner although, deep down, she was relieved. The pressure was off.

Over two months passed before Elle and Sophia got to hang out together. It was for a family gathering. Elle's dad had gotten a new job at an accounting firm, and they were going to celebrated with a barbeque in Golden Gate Park. "Finally, for once, some good news for this family," her mother said. Elle's mom had marinated baby back ribs over night and her dad had them cooking on the grill. They had claimed a spot near the rose gardens beneath a cluster of plum trees. Marcel was playing catch with Michelle and showing her some moves. Uncle Tri was playing the guitar and serenading his pretty new Thai girlfriend. Aunt Trang arrived with Dean and Sammie and some good news from Frank's lawyer. Aunt Kim arrived hugging a bucket of KFC chicken legs and a container of slaw.

She said, "I knew no one would remember to bring the American food if I didn't." But Elle knew the truth. Aunt Kim was plain tired and Vietnamese food took forever to make.

Elle ran up and offered to unload the food. Her aunt greeted her with bluish bags beneath her eyes. Elle asked, "Where's Sophia?"

Aunt Kim shrugged her shoulders as if she had given up even trying and then said, "She said she might be late."

And then as if on cue, Sophia roared up on the back seat of a motorcycle with her long black hair flapping in the wind. Elle watched Sophia dismount and then hug the guy good-bye. Sophia looked beautiful. She wore a blue floral sundress that pinched at the waist and a red scarf around her neck that made her look sophisticated and chic.

When they stood face to face, Elle said, "Miss you." Sophia didn't say it back.

Then Elle said, "Cute scarf," which got Sophia's attention. Sophia gave her a mischievous grin and then looked over both shoulders. When she was sure none of the adults were looking, she untied the knot at her throat. Beneath the red scarf, she revealed three hickeys the size of robin eggs above her collarbone and below her earlobe.

Sophia bit her bottom lip. "Motorcycle man gave them to me. Do you remember him? The hot older guy from The Steps of Rome? Can you believe it? He's crazy. He has these three boas at his apartment he keeps in the kitchen. He let me feed it a mouse last night."

Elle wanted to ask, "How old is he?" But she didn't. She didn't want to dim the glorious light in Sophia's eyes.

They spread out the food and all the fixings on the checkered tablecloth. Elle lifted the plastic lid from the red and white bucket and a waft of steam fogged up her sunglasses. There was enough fried chicken to feed an entire village. They dished the coleslaw, mashed potatoes and gravy, and corn bread on to their paper plates. Elle's mom saw the fast food and said with a tone of barely hidden disdain, "Don't spoil your appetite with that stuff." Her mom's gaze shifted to the spring rolls, lemongrass chicken, and the papaya salad she'd spent two days preparing.

"Oh my God, it's so bad," Sophia said reaching into the bucket, "but I can't help it. I love it."

"Me too," said Elle. She gave her cousin a wink. Even though she loved her mom's cooking best, today Elle reached for the fried chicken too. She said, "Do you think it's good in a bad way? Or bad in a good way?"

Sophia said, "I think it just hurts so good."

The girls bared their teeth and bit into the drumsticks at the same moment. The fried meat was succulent and juicy. The golden batter was crispy and hot. A layer of oil dripped down their fingers and lips while the girls glistened beneath the sun.

ARCADE GAMES

The surface of beauty is awful and enormous to all of us
who are left behind and yet we seek our coordinates, willfully
follow them just the same as the moon might seem from certain
angles to willfully follow the earth.
— Jennifer Moxley, "Fear of an Empty Life"

Michelle was tying her hair in a ponytail about to go for a swim when he walked up and asked, "*Oye, morena, ¿quieres nadar?*"

"I don't speak Spanish," she said.

"Aahh, *americana*," he said. "You like swim?" and began carving his arms through the air in sharp swimming strokes. The sides of his torso flared out like wings. She could imagine a jet stream trailing behind in his wake. Suddenly, he put both hands to his throat and made himself go cross-eyed. He stuck out his tongue. It was the color of her favorite bubble gum. She laughed, covering her mouth the way her mother had taught.

He repeated, "Swim yes?" When he kneeled on the edge of her towel she noticed the glaze of salt on his browned skin.

"Michelle!" She heard her name being called but pretended she didn't hear it.

"*Mi cariño*," he said and stroked her cheek with the back of his hand. The salt granules scratched a fine line across her face.

She was fifteen and for the first time in her life wondered what a man must taste like.

"Michelle!" Her mother was screaming from down the shoreline. Michelle wondered what she would think of her mother if she didn't actually know her. Huong Le, the consummate beauty, the one-time refugee, the mother of two daughters, the recent divorcee. Her mother was dressed in white from head to toe. Her silk blouse and linen trousers flapped in the breeze. She came forward looking like a majestic sail boat parting through a sea of oiled limbs.

When she arrived she said, "Michelle, where've you been? I've been looking everywhere. Everyone's waiting on you." Her mother eyed him and asked, "Was he bothering you?"

Michelle said, "Nuh-uh," as she watched him laying his towel down only a couple of feet away. It was embarrassing how her mother always spoke in loud Vietnamese.

"Well, you shouldn't speak to strangers. And why didn't you come when I called?" She looped her finger around the strap of Michelle's bathing suit and moved it aside to inspect the tan line. "You've gotten awfully dark," she said.

"I don't mind," said Michelle.

"It makes you look common. Like some sort of peasant or a field worker or something."

Some boys ran up to him as if they knew him. He talked to them but Michelle saw that he was watching her above their heads. She said to her mother, "I've been told my tan looks nice." His watching had pushed her to be brave.

Her mother said, "It's fashionable to look poor only if you're not." Her mother stretched the strap even further, once peeking down Michelle's chest, and then let it snap. "Come on," she said, "let's go."

She wanted to tell her mother she was wrong. But she knew

better. She knew her mother would slap her, say *Children obey*. She didn't want to be humiliated in front of him.

While Michelle packed up her things he came and stood beside her. They didn't say anything to each other. They watched her mother down at the water wiggling her toes in the sea foam. Her mother took off her white hat and fanned herself with it. She smoothed down her hair, tucking a shiny lock behind one ear. Her skin was so fair it was almost blue, opalescent. In Vietnam, this had meant something.

The strappy sandals dangling from her mother's fingers shimmered like silver fish hanging on a line. The man pointed to Michelle, then at her mother and said, *"¿Son hermanas?"*

Michelle shook out her towel with such disgust she blasted sand in her own eyes.

Her mother screamed up, "Let's go! Your aunt Kim's waiting!"

On the way back to the *pensión* her mother said, "Your habitual lateness is ill-mannered. It's disgraceful. No way for a lady to act."

"Sorry."

"I didn't slave and save to spend my entire vacation always looking for you, always baby-sitting."

"What's the big deal?"

"Big deal? You and your father are the same. People born in the year of the mouse are tricky, selfishly meek. Maybe if we'd had another cat around on this trip it would have been more balanced."

Michelle said, "I knew you wanted Elle to come instead."

Her mother said, "Stop it now. But why *did* your sister decide to stay home with your father this summer anyhow? It's odd to me a cat would choose a mouse over another cat."

Michelle could have said that her older sister Elle had stayed back in San Francisco to be with her new boyfriend before she had to go off to college and not because she was choosing dad. But she decided not to. She didn't want to have to take sides again. She didn't want to rehash any bit of the awful painful heartbreaking divorce between her mom and dad. Besides, tonight was their last night in Spain. Michelle couldn't stand for her mother to have another fit. It was easier with mother blaming her cursed destiny on karma: from the American War, to her divorce from father, to the sea of differences separating her from Michelle.

Later that evening, they attended an end-of-the-season dinner party hosted by the *pensión* owner for all of her employees and the dozen pensión guests. Michelle, her mother, and Aunt Kim sat at a long wooden table right beside the sea. Michelle could hear the roar of the ocean when the video arcade next door wasn't blasting its music too loud.

The hostess circled with a jug of sangría. Michelle begged her mother, *pleasepleasepleasepleasepleaseplease*. Her mother's hand didn't budge from the top of her glass. She said, "Alcohol leads to ostentation and ostentation is never attractive."

The hostess held up her glass and everyone, including Aunt Kim, shouted, *"Salud!"* Michelle asked for a sip. She wanted an orange slice or just a piece of pear. Her aunt refused, deferring to her mother. She kept hoping her aunt would stand up for her. But Aunt Kim sat docile, having grown comfortable in her invisibility, the luckless younger sister of the most beautiful girl in town.

Her mother kept putting food on Michelle's plate, selective in her choosing, prosciutto and *paella*, tuna and shrimp. She said, "You need to fatten up. Those sports have made you too skinny."

"Please Mother, I'm not a baby anymore."

Her mother said, "Only babies return kindness with ungrate-
fulness." And this was when the beautiful man from the beach
arrived. Michelle couldn't believe he was here and wondered if
he was an employee or a guest. He sat down right next to her
mother. She was still holding the shrimp platter so she turned to
him and said in English, "Do you want some?"

He nodded and her mother served.

Her mother said, "This is excellent too. Would you like
some?" He nodded and put his hands together like a prayer. Her
mother ladled a mound of saffron rice on his plate, making sure
to top it with mussels.

The man asked her mother, "You *Americana*, yes?"

"San Francisco," she said.

"It's beautiful?"

Mother told him it was mostly inconvenient. She described
the hilly streets and windy roads, the traffic she deplored. He
listened so hard crease marks formed on his brow. Finally, he
shrugged his shoulders. "*Perdón*, I don't follow."

Her mother pursed her lips, paused, and then asked, *"Parlez-
vous français?"*

"Bien sûr," he replied.

He looked older in the night but Michelle couldn't decide
how old. His hair looked darker because it was damp and
combed off his face. He wore clean white trousers and a white
shirt with wooden buttons.

The three of them sat in a row on the same side of the table
with Michelle, then her mother, then the man at the very end of
the corner. Her mother sat in the middle and was blocking him,
so Michelle didn't realize it when he spoke to her for the first
time. He had to lean forward with his elbows on the table and he
said, "I am Luis Garrigos. I see you at the *playa, no?*"

Michelle could think of nothing to say.

In English her mother said, "This is my daughter, Michelle."

"Ah, beautiful girl," he said.

Her mother brushed Michelle's hair away from her mouth and said, "Oh, she's okay."

"You like swim?" he asked.

"She should stay out of the sun. Look how dark she is," her mother replied.

"You enjoy Javea?" he asked.

Michelle blurted "I love it, I love the ocean!" She was sick of her mother answering for her. But she also feared her mother's blabbing (as she had been throughout the ten days) about how it was her first all-girl vacation, or how she could barely afford it, or how she had picked the Costa Del Sol based on a tarot reading the day she filed for divorce.

He said to Michelle, "You love? Americans love too easy?" It made her blush.

Aunt Kim sat across from them as if she were an audience watching a scene unfold. Her aunt smiled with her teeth stained gray from the red wine and her face like a plum, flushed after a few sips of alcohol. Michelle was glad that Aunt Kim had joined them after what her mom described as, "a really bad year in a string of bad years."

Mother was referring to Sophia's news that she was pregnant. The father was some older biker guy who claimed that he could support Sophia and the baby. But Aunt Kim was doubtful, she didn't like his slacker looks. She said that the few times they met, "He had on the same pair of jeans with the same discoloration at the crotch."

Luis' mouth was tinted the color of smashed raspberries. He offered her mother wine. Her mother refused it. But he said something and Michelle's mother who practically never drank alcohol allowed him to pour. Even Aunt Kim lifted her brows.

Her mother and Luis talked to each other in French. It sounded like birds chirping, brisk and zooming, as if it were a conversation carried on in flight. They only landed when Luis stopped to eat. He tore a piece of crusty bread, ate some, and placed some of it on her mother's plate. Her mother licked the tip of her finger and dabbed up the crumbs, nibbling at them one by one. Then her mother turned to Aunt Kim and reported, "He's going to be a doctor. He starts medical school come fall." She sipped her wine. "He works for the hostess in the summers to save for school. He lifeguards and gives sailing lessons." She whispered these details even though she was speaking in Vietnamese. "Poor thing, no father and he's the oldest of five boys to boot."

Luis filled her mother's glass with more wine and then they were off again, soaring in their own language. It occurred to Michelle that Aunt Kim must have also spoken French, but nobody bothered to include her. Her aunt asked Michelle, "Please, will you pass me the wine?"

Once her mother started drinking, she didn't notice anyone but Luis. Michelle shook her mother's elbow. "Did you know a psychic told me that I was a flamenco dancer married to a famous bull fighter in a past life?" She elbowed her mother's side. "Did you know that García Lorca organized the first *cante jondo* around here?" She tapped her shoulder. "Can we go to Dénia before the airport?" She tapped her knee. "I want to buy those special leather bags for the other girls on my softball team."

Her mother said, "No," "No," and "No." She even said it with her French accent. Her mother's dark hair and dark almond eyes glowed beneath the moonlight. It was a striking contrast against her translucent complexion in the night.

The sea murmured. Luis looked mesmerized. He served her mother a piece of flan. Her mother pushed it away. He nudged it forward. She scooted it back. Their fingers brushed once. The dessert quivered.

Michelle said, "I'm gonna go call Dad now." She was disappointed when her mother said nothing, no argument, no concern or jealousy, no flash-fire fury.

Aunt Kim heard and put down her steak knife. She reached for her coin purse, and from across the table rattled it in Michelle's face. "There's enough there for America," she offered.

Michelle said, "I might as well wait. Dad's picking me up from the airport anyway." Aunt Kim complimented Michelle on being a reasonable girl and then she told her to eat more since the food was free.

Her mother overheard and said, "You want more? Help yourself. Don't be shy." She scooted over the platter of *paella*. "Look, there's still plenty of shrimp," she smiled and widened her eyes.

Michelle put her elbows on the table and puffed out loud.

"You're acting up. What's wrong?"

"Nothing," she said.

Her mother placed her hands on both sides of Michelle's cheeks. Her fingers were warm and smooth, thin as paper. "Smile, I hate to see you so mopey. It's our last night. If you like, you can go to the arcade. Would you like that?" She swiveled Michelle's chin in the direction of the music. The time had arrived when the arcade became a disco. Shrill whistles and bouncy synthesizers pumped out of the white-washed bungalow next door to the *pensión*.

On their first day, her mother had said, "Who knows what kind of riff-raff congregate in there," and forbade her from going. Now her mother in Luis' presence gave her money and pushed her along. "Here's some extra. Treat the hostess' daughter too if you see her."

Everyone at the dinner table was now red from either too much sun or too much drink or both. Some screamed to talk over the music while others leaned in very close to speak. Her mother and Luis were eating from the same plate, sharing the flan.

Michelle tossed her napkin on the table and sprinted to the disco-arcade next door. When she entered, the music was so loud, it felt like she had passed through a force field. Her face tingled from the booming speakers She tried to recall the gestures of cool come-hither posturing that made her sister so popular with the boys. She attempted to imitate her mother's smile. The local boys surrounded her. They bought her Coca-Colas and told her jokes she barely understood. A blonde boy everyone called Rubio bought her two sodas and said, "I find you pretty."

She sat in a booth with Rubio and his friends. They asked her questions about American bands that were popular many years ago. She wondered what sophisticated things Luis was talking with her mother about in French. Rubio banged his elbow when he reached for her knee. She yawned and he said, "No more party? But Americans like party. Come on, we dance." Michelle said she didn't like the song. He said "You can choose," but at the juke box he picked the songs himself.

Rubio led her into a back room with flashing strobe lights and lipped-locked couples swaying on the dance floor. The music was fast but their bodies moved slow. He said, "Let's dance," and immediately reached for her butt using both hands. The disco ball flashed a rainbow stripe across his cheek. She aimed for it when she slapped him with a *twak!*

She marched away passing people squished so close their

bellies touched. The bar's beer signs flickered on and off casting shadows on panting silhouettes. Clusters of couples wiggled behind curtains of beads and steam. Michelle wondered what it was like to be kissed. She was the last of her friends because she had always been a tomboy and a late bloomer. She wanted her first kiss to be like it was in the movies and she determined this summer would be it.

In the corner of the room, she played a video game called *Galaga*. It was difficult to concentrate. She was distracted by a couple making out next to the bathroom. Another one of her spaceships had died when someone arrived and breathed over her shoulder.

"*Hola americana.*"

"Buzz off," she said.

He leaned in a bit closer. "*¿Cómo estás?*"

"*Mal,*" she said.

"*¿Por qué?*" He put his hands above her head on either side of the video console.

"*Porque,* I don't like you," she said. She was pounding on the fire button. Her elbow jabbed his gut. She didn't care.

"*¿Por qué?*" he insisted. She finally gave up and turned to leave. She smacked straight into Luis. His chest smelled of burned wood, cigarettes, and sea air.

"*Mira,*" he said. He took her by the shoulders and faced her to the screen. She wanted to show off for him but she was so nervous she instantly died.

"I try," he said. He put his hand over hers. They glided with the movement of the spaceship. His legs wedged into the nook behind her knees. They screamed when the multi-colored invaders attacked.

He shouted, "Oh my God! Oh my God! No, No, No!" She laughed throwing her head back and knocked him in the chin.

She felt so bad about it that without thinking, she reached for his face to apologize when the stubble of his jaw shocked her.

When their last man blew up, Luis slammed his fist against the control panel. He shouted at the Martians, cursing them and their *madres*. His theatrics cracked her up, but this time she stopped mid-laugh, because he had paused, and in the stillness, stared at her as if he wanted to devour her.

He asked, "Again?"

She said, "Nah, you stink," and rolled her eyes. She was too embarrassed to say she had no money left.

Luis petted her head and left her standing alone at the game. She watched his sun-streaked head bobbing toward the middle of the room. He was taller than most of the kids and stooped slightly above the crowd, accustomed to being a tall man in a not so tall country. Then he stopped to talk to somebody, combing his fingers through his hair as if he was self-conscious. He spoke to a girl sitting on one of the stools. Michelle saw that she had long black hair that ended at her tucked-in waist. He whispered in her ear and then tipped his beer bottle in the girl's direction before disappearing into the crowd. The girl giggled and threw her hair back. But then the girl turned, and Michelle couldn't believe it.

She marched up and asked, "Why did you change? Whose jacket is that?" She had never seen her mother act this way before.

Her mother said, "I didn't change. I got cold and the hostess lent me her jacket." Michelle said, "Why are you here?"

"Calm down, Michelle. I'm here same as the others. What does it look like? I'm vacationing." Recently, it seemed as if her mother had completely changed as a result of the divorce. She acted youthful and haughty, a return to her school-girl glory days. She even spoke differently, affected, with a different cadence or diction or a tone that had bite with each word.

Michelle was so upset she hadn't even noticed Aunt Kim. When she looked around, she saw that the hostess and the rest of the dinner party had migrated there too.

Her mother swatted at Michelle's long billowy skirt, "You've got bread crumbs on yourself." Her eyes were glassy and her breath smelled of alcohol. "Come closer, here," she said, "the straps are uneven." She began untying the bow on Michelle's shoulder. Michelle stepped back and held on to the front panel over her chest. Her mother reined her in and whispered, "Stay still. Nobody's looking. Besides, you've got nothing to show." She was drunk and took her time fumbling with the straps. She was brushing nothing in particular off of Michelle's shoulders when Luis all of a sudden returned.

He stood between them and put his arms over each of their shoulders. He swayed his hips back and forth to the beat of strumming guitars. Over the music he shouted, "Come on play!" They didn't know what he was talking about. He pointed to the other room with the mouth of his bottle. He moved his elbow back and forth like the wheels of a choo-choo train. When she craned her neck, Michelle saw the edge of a pool table.

Her mother said, "Do you mean billiards?" She put up both hands to refuse. "No not me. You two go ahead," she said. "I'll watch from here." But Michelle knew that all one could see from where she sat was the corner pocket.

Luis said, "I wait," and pointed his head toward the other room.

Michelle was about to follow when Aunt Kim said, "Be careful little one."

Her mother said, "Oh *please*." Her lips tumbled over each other and sputtered the words "please."

Aunt Kim said, "He's like a fox in a hen house with you

two around."

Her mother said, "And how would you know?"

She sipped more wine and closed her eyes. When she reopened them, she looked at Michelle the way she did when they were in dressing rooms together. She surveyed from head to toe and back again before taking a deep breath. "This one is a mouse," she said, "She takes after her father." She spit out the F of the "father," like a venomous dart, a needle, a sting. "Go on," she said and shooed Michelle away.

In the billiard room, Luis held out a pool stick at arm's length. It stood taller than her. Michelle said, "But I don't know how to play."

He put the colored balls in a triangle. He hit them hard and they broke apart. He showed her how to do the same. It felt unnatural when he put the cue between her thumb and the knuckle of her index finger.

Luis helped with her alignment. He guided her elbows and positioned her hips. He pushed her parallel to the floor, a palm between the shoulder blades, sometimes a little more. She giggled and he scolded. She was nervous and he was all nerve. The wooden buttons of his shirt dug in her back.

When only the eight ball was left, he unwrapped himself and said, "OK, I watching you."

Although she had memorized his instructions, she would stiffen each time she bent over the table. What would her mother think if she could see her now? Taking on these poses in front of a man? Michelle went to the far end of the room. She spied around the corner and watched her mother doing a shot with the hostess and Aunt Kim. The three women made faces like they'd tasted bitter-melon.

The other patrons in the pool room had disappeared in the dark. Luis sat beneath a beer sign, his head against the wall.

From the shadows he called out, "What, you no like to play?" Beneath the red light he was headless. He was a bright white outfit. One hand clenched around the bench. The other hand wrapped around the neck of a beer bottle.

She missed the shot again and again. "Sorry." She blushed.

"No," he said, "no, you are good *estudiante*, continue."

When she made the final shot, the white ball went in with the black. She knew it was wrong and apologized again. He said, "It's okay." He tapped the bench inviting her to sit beside him. When she sat down, he slid sideways just in time so that she landed on his lap.

She felt like a doll with her feet swinging above the floor. He kissed her cheek and then he kissed her shoulder. He bit her earlobe. It made her shriek. "Shhh…" he said, making her meek.

He said *"Que bella,"* hot to her ear. He slurred *que bella que bella*, over and over, until all the bells clanged together and she realized he was very drunk.

She said, "Maybe we should stop. What about my mom?"

He said, *"No pasa nada, chica."* His nose was buried in her hair and he lifted her skirt from behind.

She said again, "What about my mom?" A chill drifted up her back. "I thought you liked her. Don't you like her?" She heard him unzip his fly. A hang nail caught on the cotton of her panties.

His scuffed brown shoes dug into the cement floor. She watched his heels mashing up the cigarette butts littered beneath them. She looked at the little beads of sweat that had formed on his nose. She thought about the first time they'd met and how he made himself go cross-eyed. Michelle didn't know it could happen like this, sitting in a pool hall fully-clothed. She thought you had to lie down and you had to be naked, that even socks weren't allowed.

She told herself, you don't even know his age. You can barely talk to him. She told herself, we're leaving tomorrow, it won't be worth it. She told herself, you've always said you wanted to be in love. And yet she wanted to stay for that first kiss on the mouth like it was in the movies.

Michelle imagined how they must have appeared. A passerby could see them and not suspect a thing. She was a girl sitting on a boy's lap. Her face was expressionless. Their movements were slight. The folds of her long dress draped over their bottom half. But then she thought that if a passerby did know, they wouldn't care. She was just another anonymous panting silhouette. The only person in the world to care would be her mother.

Luis moved his hips back and forth. He'd inch forward and she'd move away. He'd move back and she'd shift forward. She didn't allow him to find his target. She remembered her mother once telling her and her sister, "A sexy woman is like a star. She knows how to maintain the illusion of attainability while never quite being in reach." Finally, when he wrapped his hands around her waist and pulled her in to hold her down, she hopped off.

"¿Qué pasa chica?" He shrugged his shoulders and raised his palms in the air. His shirt was damp. It was long enough to hide himself beneath it. Sweat stains had pooled beneath his arms. He mumbled and swatted at a mosquito and cursed when he missed it. She ignored him, smoothing down her skirt and adjusting the bows on her shoulders.

"Vale," he said. He rapped on the bench with his knuckles. Knock. Knock. She wanted to say, "Who's there?" like the joke, but instead Luis' knocking was answered by a flurry of laughter skidding into the room. Ha-Ha, Ha-Ha, it sounded just like her mother hammering from the bar. *Ha-Ha, Ha-Ha,* the pounding of the final drinks. This from a woman who all her life predivorce didn't touch a drop of alcohol except for the single sip after a champagne toast.

Luis was zipping up his fly while everyone was saying their good-byes. She heard her mother say, *"Adios,"* the only Spanish she ever used.

Michelle took Luis' hand and she sat back down beside him. He pulled her in tight and said with delight, *"Ah, que bella, americana."* He cupped her face in his hands and looked at her the way he had at that first encounter on the beach. He lifted her back on his lap and finally kissed her on the lips. At last, first base, this was the position she played on the school softball team. She wanted to stay there, just kissing and kissing and kissing forever. But in the next minute, he was already moving on to second and racing the clock to slide into home.

The jukebox played an aching love song. The strum of guitar matched the deliberate footsteps she'd heard all her life. Her mother was rounding the corner. Her words swelled as she neared. Michelle tried to linger, rocking back and forth on his lap. It felt like the swaying motions of a boat. He gave sailing lessons. Her mother had told her so. And so she stayed on his lap, anticipating the tide. Michelle held her breath. If she could time it right, if she could wait another beat, maybe, just maybe, she'd get swept to shore.

IN THE SEASON OF MILK FRUIT

Ma hides a stack of old photos at the bottom of her velvet-lined jewelry box. They are hidden beneath mismatched earrings, perfume samples that will never know the inside of a wrist, old keys that open forgotten doors. The photos are from the old country, framed by those old fashioned scalloped edges and washed in a sepia haze. Still, in each one, my Ba looks like a brand new Cadillac, shiny and modern, gleaming into the view-finder.

I've only met my father through these snapshots. He's got these high cheekbones, a square jaw, thick-thick lips, and big brown eyes with lashes that curl up like a beautiful black girl's. In my favorite picture, gold tassels dangle from the shoulders of his crisp white officer's uniform. He stands in front of the U.S. Embassy and above his pomaded jet-black hair the flags dance in a tango. His officer's cap is stiff and flawless. It is held to his chest like a pledge saying, I am your humble servant. But his eyes look like he's going to eat you up if you look at him for too long. I can't help but stare and stare.

You might not see these photos for many years. You might not understand for many more. But I'm telling you, because if I keep you, maybe you'll turn out like him and you deserve to know these things. When you're kicking inside of me, I imagine you're just as stubborn as my Ba. And I'll tell you a secret, just you: your dad—he somehow looked like Ba. Same wicked smile. Same long eyelashes curling into the heavens. Same full lips that were in themselves a meal. Maybe that's why I gave it up so easily.

A psychic once told me that I would have twin boys. It was this last summer when I turned sixteen. Your aunt Elle and I decided to take a road trip across America while both our moms were away in Spain. We were like wild yearling mares, nostrils flaring, eager to stamp through life. Elle had saved enough money from her job at Chevy's to buy a banana-yellow, big as a boat, 69 Mercedes that drank only diesel. We floated past the Sierra Nevada mountains and the Southwest deserts and through an ocean of corn fields, until finally, we entered Louisiana.

In New Orleans, we ended up in a two-room shop in an alleyway off Bourbon Street that had an entire wall from top to bottom of glass jars filled with herb concoctions. On the other wall, sequined and feathered Mardi Gra masks hung in festive shades of sapphires, violets, and pinks. In a small back room, I sat on an oval-backed velvet chair across from the psychic. He sat daintily with one leg crossed over his knee and his hands folded in his lap. He asked me only for my name. Beneath the blanket of burning incense and his Drakkar Noir cologne, he told me my life story.

He said, "Sophia, in a past life you were married to a brave samurai warrior. It was the time of the feudal wars and your husband was a great regional lord. Your only son insisted on fighting beside his father although you pleaded with him not to go. Both died in battle. In this life, you will be reunited with them." He shook his head in a flourish of regret. "Sweetheart, I guess you just weren't ready to say good-bye." Then he leaned forward from his velvet chair and in a low conspiratorial voice said, "In this life, you will have twins. One will be your former son and the other will be your former husband."

I wish I had asked, What about my father in this life? Where is my Ba now? I am a dog chasing its tail.

In the very beginning, my Ba, Duc Nguyen, met my Ma, Kim Le, in the season of mangoes and milk fruit so ripe they were thudding to the ground faster than people could pick them up. Sàigòn smelled animal that year. The air was sugary-sweet and pungent like sex and sewer ladled together. People were aware of their bodies like never before: the sheen of sweat on skin, salt on the lips, the hot rub of inner thighs slapping against one another sashaying down the sidewalk. Young school girls in filmy white *áo dài* moved through the streets like flocks of doves radiant in the hot white sun. Desire made the residents of the city hungry all the time, insatiable.

It was lucky then that Ma was working at the most popular noodle shop in town. *Pho Ngon* was famous for its irresistible broth brimming with star anise, cloves, roasted onions, and most coveted, the beef bones filled with the juiciest of marrow. Ma should have been studying for her college exams but she was waiting tables that summer to make her parents mad. They were bourgeois Francophiles. They couldn't believe that their daughter would choose to be a servant and, even worse, a servant to commoners.

The restaurant was a simple street-side affair. There was a wooden counter, some plastic stools, and the open air. The patrons hovered over their bowls with their backs to the traffic. For fifteen delicious minutes they were oblivious to the smog and horns and the curses of the streets. They ate in a delirium of passion, slurping noodles and smacking their lips. They sucked the marrow out of the bones the way they wanted to inhale the best out of life. They tossed the bones to the ground once sucked dry. This, they said, is the way to live, especially when the world was in a state of such uncertainty. Stray dogs came in packs to feed at their feet. It was the kind of place so democratic anyone could go: cyclo drivers and prostitutes, merchants, and Sàigòn's chief of police.

Ba had just been crowned the city's youngest police chief and when the ladies looked at him they saw a new day. The noodle shop was his favorite eatery in the entire five-district area he canvassed. He dropped by before and after every shift. He ate pho for breakfast and lunch Monday through Friday. The waitresses whispered behind their cupped hands at how sexy he was when he ate. They liked watching him dab ever so politely at the corners of that sinful mouth.

My father had his pick and he picked my Ma. "Because I fed his hunger," she says. She always says it with a sly smile like she smells something fragrant in the air that nobody else can smell. I imagine him on tipped toes reaching through leaves to pluck that singular perfect milk fruit. It hangs from a weighted branch, a sweet deep purple, the same shade my nipples have become now heavy with you. In Vietnamese, milk fruit is called *vú sua*, which translated means breast milk.

Ma was seven months pregnant with me when she kissed my Ba good-bye for the last time. He was off to fight a campaign near an area now called the Ho Chi Minh trail. Older brother Marcel was three and a terror even then. He was kicking at her ankles and begging to go to battle with Ba. Meanwhile, I was kicking harder than a mule with a burr in its ass. She put his hand on her swollen belly and with those broad fingers he caressed me with the lightness of butterfly wings. He kneeled down and whispered something Ma didn't hear. It was a prayer or maybe a poem, whatever it was, she says, "Like a salve you settled back into your cocoon."

"I think you wanted to come out and say hello or good-bye?" Ma says it in a question with her famous sad eyes and defeated smile. He didn't come back after that.

On the last day I was in his presence, he was wearing that officer's uniform, pressed and starched. His movie star looks fooled Ma into thinking that it wasn't real. She had lived in the shadow of her older sister, Huong the beauty, her entire life. It had led her to believe that beautiful people don't die. In fact, it appeared that such beauty made you invincible. Later she said, "And I was right because he didn't die. He just ended up in prison which was the same as dying."

Ma started with the drinking after their missed reunion. She had waited ten years for it. Finally, after keeping my brother and I fed and off the streets, after keeping her legs closed for all those years, after saving all that money, waiting in those lines, filling out those forms, he was finally arriving. She'd bought a potted orchid for her bedroom and some ferns to hang in the kitchen. She was scrubbing down the apartment every second she could spare away from work. I remember because she gave Marcel the whooping of his life for stomping through her freshly mopped floors with his muddied baseball cleats. She even went to Walgreen's to buy new make-up when before she used to say, "I don't have time for that foolishness."

Ma signed us up for summer camp that year. She wanted a week alone with Ba without us kids around to play spy. She dropped us off on her way to the airport. Ma was all nerves like a teenager again. She had her hair done up with just a few loose tendrils framing her face and the black liquid eyeliner that made her look like a cat. She was beautiful. I was scared to go away but didn't want to ruin it by crying. I stuffed my face in my rolled up sleeping bag. I bit my cheek hard as I could, praying the hurt would chase away the fear. Ma gave me a kiss and called me my favorite nickname. She said, "Dumpling, you'll love it. You're going to have so much fun you won't want to come back. But when you do come back, we'll be one big happy family." I let the red smack of her new L'oreal lipstick linger on my cheek as a seal to the promise. I left it there for an entire day and a night until the camp counselors got mad and told me to wash up proper.

Camp wasn't too bad though it was a different world from the city. In our neighborhood, I fell asleep to the steady chop of helicopter blades on ghetto birds. Drunken whoops in the night meant there was a party or a fight but certainly a sign of life outside our apartment walls. Ambulance sirens were a reminder that someone was rushing to help someone else out. At camp, there was just a lot of open air. I had never been around so many trees all in one place before. At night, it was pitch black and so quiet it was eerie.

At first, I couldn't go to the bathroom at night because you had to go down a trail to an outside shared bathroom. Finally, when a girl from our cabin went with me, she said it was weird that I would look over my shoulder all the time. I thought it was weird she didn't. I had picked the biggest and heaviest flashlight to double as a weapon just in case someone was there to jump us. By the end of camp, I didn't watch my back as much. I noticed that difference the most.

I liked the part on survival skills best. They showed us how to forage for things to eat if we were ever stuck outside overnight. I liked stepping into a lake for the first time too. Mud squished between my toes while I watched tadpoles scatter like dandelion seeds every which way. The camp counselors taught

us arts and crafts. We threaded jasmine together to make bracelets, garlands, and crowns. On the last night, some of the girls
wore their garlands to sleep so that the sweet jasmine enveloped
them inside their sleeping bags as they dreamed of being forest
fairies and wood nymphs. I saved mine in a Ziploc bag so that I
could give it to Ma as a present.

I didn't need the fairytales anymore. I had my fantasy
to come home to. Marcel and I would race up the stairs with
our sunburned noses and discover a new life. That was when
the real fun would start. My Ba would pick me up from school
and everyone would see that I had a father. He would meet my
teacher at Open House and she would say what a good singer I
am. He would not smile but nod, stern and proud just like he is
in the photo.

When the day came, Ma and Ba didn't pick us up at the bus
station as promised. Aunt Huong came with Elle and Michelle
instead. I knew something was wrong when Auntie didn't even
criticize us for getting dark. She didn't call us "Indians," or
"slaves." She didn't say, "If your father were here, he would kill
your mom for letting you get so dark that you look like a peasant." She faked a cheery smile the whole ride home and before
dropping us off said, "Be good to your poor Ma." It prepared us
for the closed curtains, browned ferns, the sink sky high with
dirty dishes, the mom with no make-up, the house with no dad.

Ma was sitting on the couch in the dark staring at the blank
screen of a TV. She said he never arrived.

Marcel said, "Stop messing with us. Where is he?" We ran
through the apartment switching on all the lights.

Ma said, "Have you kids gone mad?"

Marcel and I swung open closet doors, pulled coats off
of hangers, pulled sheets from the bed, threw blankets to the
ground. We crawled under the bed, spitting out the hair in our

mouth, behind the fridge rubbing the cobwebs from our eyes, beneath the kitchen sink, inside the tub. We pillaged the house screaming, *"Ba oi! Ba oi!"*

Ma screamed back, "He's not here."

I scowled at her. "Liar liar pants on fire!"

We kept at it for over an hour until we were exhausted by our own rage, until I found myself looking for him in the reflection of a plate, at the bottom of a tea cup that instead caught my tears, and when I returned to the plate and only saw my myself, I smashed the plate into pieces I could swallow.

Ma held me down. Spit flew from her mouth even though her voice was not raised. She said, "Look at you, a big baby who can only think of herself. Did you ever think of me? Once?" She let go of her clutch and flung me away like a used up piece of paper. Her hands were frozen in the air, palms inches from my shoulders as if an electric force field separated her and me. I'd seen it on the street. Two guys are about to fight and one does that frozen hands mid-air gesture that says you're such a piece of shit you're not even worth my time.

The answer was I did and I had thought about her. I ran for my backpack and reached for the Ziploc bag. I draped the garland around her neck. Again the sad-eyed weak smile. She lifted a handful of blossoms to her nose and smelled them. She said, "White flowers are for the dead."

Later, Ma explained that the Communists had held him back. He was at the gates of Tan San Nhat airport when the pig-nosed official took a look at his documents and refused him passage. Ba felt for the razor in his back pocket and imagined himself slicing off that nose. They recognized his name, Duc Nguyen. His reputation preceded him. He was the great soldier from the South, the one who had fought shoulder to shoulder beside the

Americans; the traitor who "betrayed your own brothers for the white imperialists." It didn't matter that he had already served his time, had been tamed and tortured for a decade in their jails. It was as easy as a swivel of the head, to the right, then to the left, not even a word, not even enough of a gesture to move the air in the hot stuffy room to crush all those years of dreaming.

There was evidence of him everywhere in our apartment. I found a man's shaving brush in the medicine cabinet and a sterling silver Zippo lighter beside the windowsill. When I presented my finds to Ma, she said, "You should be in theater. You have quite the imagination. That's your uncle's." It was obvious though when she kept the lighter and took up smoking. She caressed the heavy lighter in her small fist like a precious stone. She sat alone at the kitchen table and flicked the fire on and off on and off until her thumb became callused and slightly charred. She stared beyond the light to the branches slapping the kitchen window. She talked to nobody in the chair beside her but the shadows of the leaves. That's when Ma began to toy with danger.

It was as if we lived with a ghost. Everyone knew he had been there but we had to pretend he hadn't. How else to explain the missing handles on her favorite teacups? The ones that were real china etched with blue vines on white porcelain. They had cost an entire Christmas bonus though she indulged anyway. Ma said that they made her feel pampered and beloved again. It reminded her of Sunday afternoon tea times with her Francophile mother in a garden blooming with red roses and green limes.

I held the damaged teacup to the sun. "What happened?"

She said, "I've turned into a clumsy old lady I guess."

When I went to the bathroom, I saw a crack on the toilet seat between my legs. I led her in and pointed. "Who did that?"

Ma got on her knees and pretended to examine the fracture as if she had not noticed it before. She placed a lock of hair behind her ear so that it won't fall into the water as her finger traced the edges of the fault line. I pleaded, "You wouldn't have needed to lift it up to go."

She said, "How would you know? Aren't I both the man and the woman in this household?"

I know it was him. I can see his blunt fingers, nails cut to the flesh, the same hand that held that officer's cap, stubborn and proud, I'd recognize it anywhere. The veins are pumping and with all his force he slams down that lid until it shattered. He pissed over the rim and it infuriated him. It reminded him that he's nothing more than an animal. He wanted to spray all over her bathroom to mark his territory but didn't bother. This wasn't territory he wanted to claim anyway.

She had tried to tame him with her biscuits and tea, her dainty cups and saucers. Instead, they crumbled under his touch. She showed him photos of children he didn't recognize. It was yet another life where he would have to amputate a part of himself to survive. He was already a man with only nine fingers and nine toes. He was incapable of being retrained and retamed and knew it. He didn't want to disappoint her anymore than he already had. She had such big dreams for him. He had touched her hope on his fingertips. The metal shavings of the brand new key she had made for his arrival flaked like dust to the ground. So he placed the key on the kitchen counter. He closed the door behind him and set out for the streets.

After what he's lived through, I don't blame him.

Except for the nights, he chokes my dreams and I can't move.

Except for the evenings, I seek him in other men.

Except for the man I foolishly hope to see in you.

The psychic said my husband and son from a past life will be born to me in this life. They were warriors who died in battle. The psychic was close but not entirely right. I was conceived in warfare, raised in a refugee camp, and came up in an urban combat zone. I am a soldier. I am a survivor. Ba isn't dead. He is only wounded. You and me baby boy, together will be a we, the search party reunited to find him.

RELIEF

M y mom and I return to Vietnam for the first time in seventeen years to see Baby Boy. He's my mom's niece's two-year-old son. I don't know what that makes him to me. Just that he's a baby that can supposedly read and because of this everyone thinks he's a miracle. Some even believe that he could be a reincarnated holy person.

My mom reminds me, "He's the most famous person in our entire family. Baby Boy's been on Vietnam's version of *Entertainment Tonight*. They've dubbed him Buddha Baby." She used to swear that she would never return as long as the country was still under Communist rule. In the end, it only took a celebrity, which says something about how American even she's become.

After only two hours in the old country, I've become a bit deaf. The first thing I learn is that they honk to let each other know where they're at. In America, we honk to say, hey, you're in the way, *Beep!* A lone somewhat embarrassed honk daring to disrupt the morning commute. But here, all six million people seem to be honking simultaneously. Cyclo drivers and cabdrivers, the ox cart driver with his two-bit horn, everyone's honking to say, I'm here, I'm here, *Honk! Honk! Honk! Ok, I'm changing my mind, now I'm over here!*

Here is officially called Ho Chi Minh City though my family defiantly calls it Sàigòn. My mom says, "I escape by boat to return and instead drown in a sea of sound." The entire city is zipping around. If you're not using one of the above-mentioned modes of transportation, you're on a scooter. Candy colored Hondas and Yamaha, Suzukis and Vespas swoosh by, cutting and skimming each other. It's like being at a football stadium while an off-key marching band plays its collective heart out and a low flying jet is hovering overhead. The roar is constant. It pulsates. I feel it on my face. It's like standing too close to the speakers at a show.

While the bellboy shows my mom the room, I run out to the hotel balcony. Our room faces the main strip. We're right across the street from the Continental. I remember it from that famous PBS documentary. The one where all the ambassadors and hot-shot journalists are sitting around smoking Gauloise cigarettes and sipping iced coffees right before Sàigòn fell. This was seconds before the choppers started coming in and air lifting people away.

I have an uncle who's considered lucky because he was a translator so he got hooked up and lifted away. Not like the unfortunate cousin who has an elbow that hangs at an odd angle from trying to scale up the American embassy rooftop. Not to mention the cursed cousin. Family legend has it that he was once a beautiful female impersonator. This was before he tried to seduce an American officer into marrying him. His twice broken nose now makes him less delicate, less beautiful. Or so I've heard. I wish my mom would tell me the rest of the story.

After all the stories I've heard, I'm dying to get to know this place better. I want to eat pho for breakfast, bike in the countryside, sail beneath the jade mountains of Ha Long Bay, eat mangos at the beach. When night falls I'm still on the balcony daydreaming and watching the streams of light zigzagging the streets. The air is electric here. I close my eyes, face tingling and think, wow, Vietnam's like a Van Halen concert, wet, steamy, thunderous.

My mom's more easy listening than rock-n-roll, so after the first sleepless night we move away from the city center. Each time we hop into a cyclo, we negotiate the price first. We've learned there are local prices, foreigner prices, and *viet-kieu* prices. When I'm charged the *viet-kieu* price I say, "How do you know I'm not local? I was born here." I watch a triad of girls linked by the arms walking toward us. They are dressed as I am, in low rider jeans, a tight t-shirt, and platforms.

The cyclo driver follows my gaze and then looks over my outfit. He says, "It's not what you wear. It's how you wear it." I had imagined my return as a homecoming. Instead it's as if he works for *Vogue* and has called out my counterfeit purse and faux labels. I fold my arms and lean back into the seat. The hinges squeak. To rub it in he says, "I can tell by the way you walk, the way you talk, the way you chew your gum in the crowd."

We leave behind the crowds, the McDonalds, the Japanese electronic stores, the shiny facades of Clinton's *doi moi*. My size-zero *fashionista* cyclo driver peddles us and our luggage through the skeleton of the city. The busy downtown area is lined with outdoor bars and cafés. It reminds me of Paris. Little round white plastic tables and striped umbrellas are pushed together so that people can enjoy each other's company beneath the sun. On a closer look, I see that the seats are filled solely by male patrons. I think maybe we're in the gay district. But as he peddles us from district to district, all the cafes appear the same. Rarely if ever is there a woman in sight amongst these clusters of body heat and watery beer.

I ask my mom, "Where are all the women? How come there are only men at the bars?"

She says, "In Vietnam, only prostitutes drink beer."

"That's ridiculous mother. I drink beer and I'm not a pros-
titute."

"Elle, you shouldn't drink. It looks cheap, it means you're
available."

We check out hotel after hotel, room after available room.
Each time, my mom enters, closes the curtains, shuts her eyes,
and shakes her head in disapproval when yet another honk seeps
its way through the cracks. Our cyclo driver peddles us deeper
and deeper into a maze of alleyways. Laundry lines overhead,
noodle stands on the curb, the roads so narrow cars don't fit, and
suddenly, a blanket of silence.

My mom places both fists beneath her chin as if she's pulling
up a blanket and is being tucked into bed. I plunk myself on to one
of the two single beds. From here, everywhere I look, I see my
mom's reflection bouncing from the shiny black lacquered furni-
ture. Huong Le's doppelganger is ivory skinned and bee-eyed and
looks back at me with rare approval. She stands in the middle of
the room, sucks in a deep breath, and says, "Ah, finally."

"Finally, it's warming up." The hotel concierge is bent over
the tub with her hand beneath the faucet. She wears blue flow-
ered pajamas and flip-flops. She shakes the water off and I watch
the drops splatter against her knee. There's a wet bloom where
she wipes her hand. A band of pale skin reveals itself when the
elastic waist of her pants gives. She flushes the toilet. It's modern
and porcelain and the water swirls and drains just fine except
there's no seat to lift up or set down.

My mom says, "See? The flat edge is for balance so you can
squat easily on top of it. Elle, don't cringe, it'll give you wrin-
kles." My mom is examining herself in the bathroom mirror as
she says this. She studies her face as if it's an object or a tool. She
presses her cheeks back. She has not remarried after the divorce,
although not from a lack of offers from Vietnamese men stretch-

ing up and down the California coast. Still studying her face she says, "Don't forget, you come from squatters."

My mom recounts her first classes in America. When the first wave of Vietnamese immigrants arrived in America, public restrooms began posting these "prohibited" and "how-to" signs. One had a person squatting on top of the bowl with big primate toes curved around the rim. The drawing was inside a big red circle with a big red X over it. The church volunteer who taught mom and dad and Aunt Kim and Uncle Lam how to be Americans told them this meant No! The other sign had a person sitting on the toilet as if it was an office chair with a serene expression on her face. My mom says, "One of the church people told me that squatting leads to hemorrhoids."

I consider risking hemorrhoids to have the true coming-home experience. Except I look down at my platform shoes with the ties and snaps and realize why the concierge and so many others wear flip flops.

The concierge asks my mom why we've returned. My mom says, "I have a nephew I want to see. He's a *special* baby." She's using her I have something to brag about but I'm going to be humble and not disclose it voice. I can tell she wishes the woman would guess that *the* Buddha Baby Boy of Sàigòn is her nephew. My mom smiles coyly but the concierge doesn't react. My mom says, "We live in San Francisco now but I haven't been back for seventeen years. I don't know if my own brother will recognize me."

Uncle Two is my mom's favorite big brother. She describes him as "handsome." She pauses and rolls her eyes as if in disbelief that a man can be so hot and related to her. "He was fair-skinned. And he was tall and he had this tall Roman looking nose. Everyone thought he was part French." She adds, "We're going to surprise him."

Celebration must follow surprises otherwise it's just jumping out of the dark and scaring the crap out of someone. Before we leave for the countryside, we haggle in the bustling market. My mom says that Uncle Two likes the slightly burnt crispy skin of roasted pig, so we buy a left torso. I can't decide between the boiled chicken hanging from its ankle or the roasted duck hanging from its beak. My mom says that my deceased grandfather *may he rest in peace* loved duck, so we can get that as an offering. On the other hand, my deceased grandmother *may she rest in peace* raised chickens all her life. We want her to be comfortable in her resting place and buy the chicken too.

As a tribute to our acclimation to Western levels of comfort, my mom and I charter a Mercedes minivan to take us to our destination. We sit with the air conditioning blasting our faces. The AC is up so high the pink plastic bags overflowing with food make a fluttering noise the entire drive. I think if mom had brought her flute and I had an ounce of rhythm, we could be the next big sensation in the niche of world music.

The riverbank is lined with homes high on stilts. We have to cross two provinces, two bridges, and then board a ferry to cross the Perfume River. I watch an old timer in blue trunks with tree-bark skin wade in while clutching a bar of soap in his hand. Soda cans gleam beneath the noonday sun and drift before him. Beside him, a group of women are washing leafy greens until one breaks from the bunch to swat a child for pissing in public over the pier.

Red brake lights stretch endlessly before us. Traffic is practically at a standstill. Everyone is waiting to board the ferry. The road is red and hot and dusty. Vendors wipe the layer of silt off our windows to better show off their goods. They press barbequed beef sticks and newspaper cones filled with boiled peanuts up to our window and leave oily fingerprints on the glass.

One vendor offers an English speaking newspaper wrapped in its original plastic announcing the upcoming Olympics as of three years ago. My mom says, "They're an entrepreneurial bunch." The roadside houses have wooden stakes in their front yards announcing bathroom use for a buck.

Toilet $1.00! A sign in purple magic marker smacks against my window. The bearer of the sign is a little girl with a perfectly round bowl haircut and two missing teeth. She swivels the sign so that the arrow now points toward a thatched roof shack which I assume is her house. She asks, "Do you want to go?" The little girl raises her eyebrows and widens her eyes, smiling as if it will be the most enticing thing in the world.

I can imagine her as a World Wrestling Federation girl who comes out between rounds holding a sign over her head. With the exception of her protruding belly, I can tell she will grow up to be a classic beauty. I see her on a calendar smiling from September with a caption in italics that speaks of her humble beginnings.

From the start she is gracious, reassuring, and a great hustler. "So pretty," she says as she takes my hand and helps me down from the minivan. Her pointing finger caresses my wrist and traces the circumference on the face of my shiny silver watch. As my handler, she directs me through the riff-raff and shoos the others off like flies. "I have all you need," she says in a perfectly practiced heartfelt voice.

With aching heart and clenched bowels, already I am missing America. The little girl leads me through her house and out to a shed in the back. A partition made of empty rice sacks stitched together separates the bathroom on one side from the pig pen on the other. The bathroom is a mere hole in the ground. A magazine rack is placed beside the hole. There is Michael Crichton's *Jurassic Park*, a Vietnamese newspaper, a Japanese comic book, and an Italian porno mag to choose from: a true global village.

It is almost comical when a pig's snout pokes through a tear in the partition. Sunlight filters through the thatched roof and illuminates a condom wrapper half buried beneath straw. The snout bucks at the flap and begins sniffing. The nostrils strain and contract in an attempt to inhale. I doubt its sense of smell is very sensitive. The nose is caked in something like mud but not mud. I now understand the architectural design of this structure. My people are so practical and efficient. It's no wonder that we won the war.

Back in the minivan, I say, "I'm sorry but I'm glad there was a war. Really, I just can't imagine living like this."

"That's a horrible thing to say. You wouldn't say it if you knew how our people have suffered."

"Can you imagine having all these strangers, weirdoes and pedophiles from all over the world, coming into your house to use your bathroom?"

"Elle, stop cringing. You'd stop if you knew how unattractive it looks."

"I swear I could barely go."

"Go deeper into the countryside then you'll really see. That was nothing. Out where your dad's from, do you know what the peasants do?"

When she wants to be uppity, my mom likes to point out that she was born in the city whereas my dad was born in the countryside. She proceeds to tell me about a particular process of fish farming she once saw at an Aunt Persimmon's house.

"I have an aunt named Persimmon?"

"And an uncle name Litchi. They're distant, but that's your dad's side for you, country bumpkins." She continues, "Your little sister Michelle was just born and we went up country to see your dad's people. Aunt Persimmon was old and bed bound and your father wanted to show Michelle off. By that time, we had already decided we wouldn't stay under Communist occupation much longer. For some reason, I had awful stomach cramps even after the pregnancy. Anyway, I asked the house girl to take me to the bathroom. I knew they were poor. I figured we'd have to go into an outhouse. Michelle was in my arms and I had her wrapped up in this beautiful rose-colored blanket my mom had hand knitted with silk yarn. There were mosquitoes buzzing everywhere because of this stagnant little pond out back. Over the pond, they had laid a plank. I followed the girl not really thinking about it. I figured that maybe the outhouse was on the other side of the plank."

"But it wasn't on the other side. We had reached our destination. The bathroom was right there beneath us. She was a young girl. She just pulled down her pants, and went." My mom pauses for dramatic effect. "I'm telling you she did more than urinate. After this, these bubbles suddenly rose to the surface. I looked down and saw dozens of little round white fish mouths emerging to feed." My mom made her hand like a Pac-Man mouth, opening and shutting while she makes a fish face and sucks her cheeks in. Her aspiring actress side has made a comeback after the divorce.

"Michelle wouldn't shut up. She started wailing because it was *her* feeding time. I was balanced on a piece of plywood, squatting there, and cradling her in one arm. There was no way I could have pulled my breast out. Now that would have been a balancing act. Imagine if I'd had dropped her! Can you imagine?" My mom can't help but suppress a smile. "Michelle would be darker than she already is!" The driver looks in the rear view and catches mom's eyes like a subtle *amen* to that. I can't wait to tell my little sis this seriously damaging story about her infancy.

My mom continues, "The worst part of the story is that

while I was worried about not falling off or dropping her in, the blanket was ruined. It was hanging right in that nasty pond water. It was a shame. I had to throw it away. After that, my mom, your grandmother never wanted me to visit your dad's people again."

Mom states, "The one thing I'll never forget is how they swallowed." Her eyes are glazed over as she says this with that looking out of the third eye look they talk about in yoga class. She says in a voice of awed recall, "The way their mouths opened up into these perfectly white round suctioning holes . . . ."

"Why didn't Aunt Persimmon's family just dig holes in the ground?"

"How would holes in the ground feed the fish?"

My mom clears her throat and adds, "They say the fish grow to be bigger than average that way. Right before they take the fish to market, they feed citrus rinds to them for a couple of weeks to get rid of the shit smell."

"Your story's ruined me for the next couple of years, thank you." My mom believes in the *things could always be worse* method of motherhood. I say, "What's up with the obsession with all things scatological here?"

"Scata-what?"

"Shit Mom, shit!"

"Don't get foul-mouthed, Missy." My mom crosses her arms and stares out the window giving me the silent treatment for the rest of the drive.

I'm the foul one? Everything here is contrary to everything I know. From traffic to farming, to the way one moves one's body, to the most minute bodily function, everything is backwards, and I'm the foul one? As we continue driving along the banks of the Perfume River, I realize the murky color is probably due to sediment run-off, but for now, all I can imagine is the runs.

Once we board the ferry and the minivan door opens, we happily stretch our legs. We find a spot at the front of the boat and I help my mom tie the ribbon on her sun hat. Near us a gathering of *viet kieu* men are snapping photos of each other. They are techies from Silicon Valley. They stand at the tip of the bow, their backs to the water, an arm casually draping the rail. The other popular pose is to put one foot on the platform while looking out to the horizon. It makes for a good profile shot. We all know the poses. We learned them from watching the *Titanic*. Meanwhile, the local men still sheltered from Hollywood, squat on the lower deck with their knees drawn up to their armpits. They're playing cards. Our driver is dealer.

When our driver pulls up to my uncle's house, I see a sinewy brown leg hanging from the hammock that reminds me of the roast duck hanging from my hand. It's as idyllic as I've always imagined the Vietnamese countryside to be. Paradise green patches of rice fields surround a little but charming cream-colored house. A wide porch is shaded by a mango tree. The tree is dotted by fruit the color of a sunset under which a dusty dog naps on red soil. Slowly, the dog stirs awake. When it unwinds itself, it turns out to be a woman in faded gray pajamas.

The driver slams the door of the minivan and jolts the woman to turn. She rubs her eyes. Even from our distance I see tears sliding down her cherub cheeks. She asks, "Sister Number Five? Is that you Huong?" Then she screams, "My lord, Heaven and Earth have collided!"

The man in the hammock lifts his head. He turns first to the left and then to the right. I don't see him face on yet, but I know he's the uncle we've come for with his nose like a sail. He steps out of the hammock and unfolds his long thin legs. My mom sees him and breaks into a sprint. She is weeping when they embrace. It's all so sweet and sentimental I cry too but can't participate because I've got a pig torso hanging from my right hand and a pink plastic bag full of fowl hanging from my left.

My uncle says, "Well look at you. When you left you were…" He puts a hand palm down beneath his knee. "Look how she's grown," he says.

My aunt leans into my mom and shakes her head. "She hasn't grown to look like you."

I smile and ask, "Who do I look like?"

My aunt inches closer, her big brown eyes zooming in on me. She states matter-of-factly, "You look American!"

Her glistening eyes look at me with pure delight as she sizes me up. She pinches my thigh as if she can extract apple pie, five-laned freeways, glass skyscrapers, and healthy cheerleaders from my flesh. She stuffs her face into my neck and sniffs, bestowing upon me a traditional Vietnamese kiss. "Smell so good," she announces.

She unburdens my hands of the groceries. I watch her waddle away, feet splayed outward like a duck, flip flops stirring up the red soil. My mom and uncle walk in front of me. He has his arm around my mom's shoulder. He is shirtless and with his free hand picks at a mosquito bite on the back of his neck until it bleeds.

My aunt hangs the pig torso from a hook above the kitchen sink. She then moves to the cutting block and begins her work on the duck. Her strokes are precise. She wields the butcher knife with the authority of a Quentin Tarantino heroine. She shoos away the flies that come buzzing around the sweet salty meat. Sometimes she bends her knees, one arm reaching for her flip flop like a cowboy about to draw in a spaghetti Western. The flies are smart. They flee at the mere gesture.

My uncle's calloused hands pour tea with a refinement of the surgeon he was before the war. My tea cup is white porcelain with a pink bud on the bottom. It looks like a rose petal shivering beneath the liquid. It is exquisite except for the brown ring inside the rim that won't come off even when I scratch it with my fingernail. I edge it over to show my mom the stain. The tea spills over the lip. She scowls at me and then kicks me under the table all the while apologizing franticly to my uncle. She is, however, gracious enough to swap cups with me.

My uncle says, "Welcome home!" and lifts his tea cup.

After they exchange the usual formalities, my mom says, "You wrote last time about Persimmon retiring soon? And how is her toy poodle?"

He says, "Her brother Litchi had to adopt the poodle. Persimmon passed in the spring."

"Oh," she says and continues on this line of questioning about pets. My mom believes it impolite to ask people difficult questions. Instead she inquires about one relative's German shepherd, another relative's beagle, an old friend's mini schnauzer. Each pet story seems to have a happy ending or a sad ending depending on how one looks at it. Either the dog is now gone or the person or both.

"You can either have tea or beer or both," my aunt says. She dishes up the food we brought. I'm starving but notice that the wooden chopsticks are discolored on the ends. The bowls put in front of us should be white but have turned a denture-colored yellow.

My aunt and uncle lift their bowls all the way to their chins when they eat and use their chopsticks to shovel food into their mouths. They compliment the food intermittently between gnawing at duck bones and slurping noodles. My aunt looks up perplexed and asks me, "Don't you know how to eat Vietnamese food?"

My mom says, "She's very good at eating." She pinches me under the table to urge me on. Her chopsticks reach for the duck. She places each piece one by one into my bowl. "Even in

America, I've taught her that wastefulness is a sin."

My uncle and aunt take sinful pleasure in hearing the gossip from abroad and my mom indulges them. They want to know who lives where, what jobs they have, who has a bigger place, the biggest house, what cars they drive? My uncle asks, is it true that in America each member of the family has his and her own car? Yes we nod. My aunt asks, is it true all American women have large breasts? She say, "We watch *Baywatch*, the show with those rescuers in red bathing suits at the beach."

My uncle then says to my aunt, "You've got to show them that article about Baby Boy." He points his chopsticks toward the living room. "After we eat" he says, "I'll show you. I set it aside on the coffee table over there."

Once I start eating I realize how hungry I am. It's delicious. The duck has a sweetness from the star anise that would humiliate the ducks hanging from the storefronts of San Francisco's Chinatown. The sweet buns are like clouds dissolving on your tongue. For the majority of the meal, we see each other only from the nose up.

As the evening dwindles away, my uncle takes pleasure in bragging about his first born grandson. Baby Boy is two years old, and according to them, the talk of the nation. "Even the Northerners are fascinated." He claims, "It's the human interest story of the year." I believe him. He is suddenly talking in sound bites.

"My daughter was going to town one morning like usual. She was carrying the boy in her arms. As they're passing through the market, Baby Boy started pointing to things and then out of the blue reading everything! Street signs, store fronts, food labels, the labels on food bins. Would you believe it?"

My aunt chimes in, "It's hard to believe he could read the food labels. That's got to be a stretch. Those market women must have the worst handwriting I've ever seen. *I* can barely read them."

My uncle continues, "His mom can't believe it. She grabs the first newspaper she comes upon. I think she actually asked some stranger for his paper. She set the newspaper in front of Baby Boy to test him out. And what do you know? The kid reads that too!" My uncle smacks the back of one hand into his palm.

Outside the crickets stop chirping and the wind settles. For a moment, it is absolutely silent as if everything and everyone is waiting to see how the story ends. "All the ladies at the market gathered around in amazement. Then the cyclo drivers crowded around to see what the fuss was about. It became a frenzy. Word passed through town. Everyone was gossiping about the miracle baby. The disbelievers started wagering bets against the believers. Some people said it was a scam. But the smart ones knew the truth. The monks say that Baby Boy can read because he is a reincarnated bodhisattva who has retained his knowledge from a past life."

My uncle shakes his head back and forth with a giant grin on his face. "Wait until you see the article. Imagine two whole pages about our family in the *Giai Phóng Sàigòn* Sunday paper! I've set it aside to save it in an album so that when Baby Boy grows up he'll have a record of all this."

My aunt serves us a whole mango each for dessert. Mine is ripe and juicy with whiskers that catch between my teeth. My uncle is wise to this and passes a toothpick holder around. He tells my aunt, "Boil some water for them. I bet a bath will feel good after sitting in a car all day long." His words are warbled by the probing in his mouth. He says, "I'll be quick so you two can get in," and excuses himself to go the bathroom. In the time it takes my aunt to pour a bucket of water in a cauldron and put it over the flame, I go from feeling good to feeling miserable. My stomach drops like an avalanche and I am certain the end is near. I wonder if it was the herbs. Maybe they weren't washed.

Or being washed with the local water might have done it too. I wonder if it could have been the mango. My mind goes through a list all the cooked and uncooked items I've eaten.

I go to the bathroom but my uncle isn't as quick as he said he would be. I am sweating like a pig. I ask my mom, "What's in the back yard? Is there a place where they feed fish back there? Is there a pond outside?" I am nearing an accident, about to crash. She says, "No," and returns her attention to my aunt at the sink. My mom is soaping. My aunt is rinsing. I am stuffing my pride in my pocket.

My only choice is to retrieve the plastic bags from our early market adventure. I go to the living room and hope with dishes and gossip to occupy them the women will not notice my absence. When I approach the coffee table I see the newspaper neatly folded before me. It is so well preserved that it makes a crisp smacking sound when I flip through each sheet. A bead of sweat is slowly making its way down my jaw. My veins are pumping so hard, I think my head will pop. My legs are squeezed together and I am holding my stomach. Outside the crickets and beetles are buzzing but all I hear is the rumbling of my insides.

Bent over the table, I curse the fact that I can't read in Vietnamese and pray that if indeed Baby Boy is a reincarnated bodhisattva, he will bless me by having a photo of himself appear inside the paper. It's the one article I have to preserve. I try to flip through quickly but it's impossible to make it past page five. I grab the whole thing, roll it up, tuck it under my arm.

The crescent moon and froth of stars illuminate the yard and crowns the distant tree tops with a silver halo. On my left I see the hammock and the mango tree where my aunt and uncle were napping this afternoon. On my right is the edge of my uncle's rubber tree farm. I go down the steps toward the privacy of the big leafy foliage when a toad hops out. Its shadow is looming and so greatly exaggerated by moonlight that it scares the bejesus and practically everything else out of me. Beside the porch steps, under the wide open skies, I drop my pants, spread out the sheets, and finally let loose.

I concentrate on the square of yellow light from the open kitchen window. My aunt is laughing hysterically at something my mom has said. The sound is rich and clear and rolls from both her belly and her heart. The back door squeaks open and swings shut. I hear my uncle's footsteps on the back porch. He lifts the lid of the trashcan. The sound of empty beer cans tumbling over each other cuts through the night. The dog barks. My uncle responds by playfully taunting her. "You greedy old mutt," he says. "Hear you go. You ugly old thing, what more do you want?"

She begins thumping her tail vigorously on the wooden deck. I can imagine being sniffed out, the dog howling, my uncle rounding the corner, me sitting over my ugly mess. With my pants around my knees, I shuffle like a crab over to the rubber trees. The leaves are silky and smooth which I'm grateful for until I learn that they're nonabsorbent and only smear things around. My uncle screams, "Bad girl!" Across the yard, I see the pile in plain view beneath moonlight.

In my urgency, I had laid out the entire newspaper consisting of roughly twenty sheets. I don't know why I just didn't go on the ground. I blame it on my Americanness, my silly attempt at being sanitized despite the obvious. The top ten sheets are soaked through. But my foolish heart races with the hope that perhaps the bottom sheets are salvageable. Maybe Baby Boy's article was spared. Maybe I can return the paper to the coffee table with nobody even noticing.

I scoop up the paper on both sides and hold it like a taco,

It is by far the most horrific and humiliating event of my life. Finally, I gather the paper on all four sides and then scrunch up the top like when I help my mom make wontons. This at least encloses it into a package. I lift up the bundle to put it inside a plastic bag. The sight before me is unsightly and I place it on the ground with a thud.

I brace myself, pick it up again and kneel down to study the plastic underside. His eyes are looking right back at me. The gaze is accusatory, too much to bear. The photo shows a baby sitting in a large leather armchair. He is propped on top of a behemoth encyclopedia. He is surrounded by stacks of books and masses of magazines. He is chubby-cheeked and clear-eyed with his Buddha belly protruding before him. He looks regal. There is no mistaking who he is. Even after I place everything into the pink plastic bags and seal it all up, I can still feel the heat of his stare searing through me.

After I bathe and my mom bathes. After we get fresh and clean and change into our crisp cotton pajamas. After we unpack our suitcases and bring out our shiny packaged gifts from America. After they say thank you a dozen times, and we say you're welcome a dozen more. After all of these pleasantries, my uncle says, "Now where's that newspaper article I promised you?"

When he stands over the coffee table and scratches his head, I think I will die. I hear him say, "I must be getting old." He grumbles under his breath and goes over to a banana leaf basket filled with old papers and screams to my aunt, "I hate it when you put things away without telling me."

He dumps the entire stack out. The newspapers spread out on the floor and he shuffles through them. He is on all fours and the knees of his white pajama bottoms get sooty with print. The blood on his neck from the bug bite has dried. I am watching as he searches through the papers. I have exactly what he wants. It is tucked away in a sky blue Samsonite suitcase. It is covered in shit, inside plastic bag upon pink plastic bags. He scrunches the papers in his fist and tosses them in the air. One by one, they flutter down like parachutes, completely vulnerable and exceedingly common, and still, I pray for each a safe landing.

READING GUIDE QUESTIONS

1. *Quiet As They Come* focuses on the lives of one extended family that has immigrated from Vietnam to America. What do their stories tell us about the two cultures that they straddle?

2. The book also straddles generations. Discuss the differing experiences between the parents' generation and that of the children. In particular, how do the children change from the first story in the book, where they are Vietnamese children in America, to the last, in which Elle returns to Vietnam for a visit? How do her Vietnamese relatives see her, and how does she see herself in this context?

3. The author has called this a book of "interlinked short stories." How does this genre differ from a novel, and how is it similar? Could each of these stories stand alone as a short story? What do they gain by their placement among the other stories?

4. Each of these stories is filtered through the point of view of one of the characters. What are the effects of these shifts in viewpoint? How do we see a character or a situation differently depending on who is looking? Choose a character and look at his or her depiction in several stories in order to tease out the effects of point of view. For instance, how do you see Kim in "The Pussycats" as compared to "Everything Forbidden" or "Arcade Games"?

5. The title of the book is taken from the impression Viet's co-workers at post office have of him. Why might this title encapsulate not just his story, but the collection as a whole?

6. What is the role of food, both Vietnamese as well as so-called American foods such as pizza, in *Quiet As They Come*?

7. Many of the images and objects in the book have both a literal and a symbolic meaning. Choose something in the collection that seems to have this kind of double meaning and unpack its symbolism. For example, in the final story, "Relief" there are multiple reference to excrement. What do all of these references—which Elle refers to as a scatological obsession—mean, at a deeper level?

8. Chau is masterful at bringing her stories to a resonant conclusion. Study the final paragraphs of several of the stories in *Quiet As They Come* with an eye toward analyzing the different ways in which Chau constructs her endings.

ACKNOWLEDGEMENTS

For their monumental support, I would like to thank Hedgebrook for the solace and fresh air, the Macondo Foundation for your community and inspiration, and to the UC Davis Creative Writing Program, where I was fortunate to have been taught by Pam Houston, the best reader I know, and Lynn Freed who instilled discipline in the best way; to Robin Romm for the great honor of selecting me for the UC Davis Maurice Prize in Fiction along with John Lescroart for making it possible; a heartfelt thanks to my reader, writer, friends, Stephan Clark, Diana Ip, Leslie Larson, Alix Schwartz, and Adam Scott for your conversation, keen insight, and beautiful minds; for his encouragement from the very start, my editor in Kauai, Dennis Wilken; to Sandra Cisneros for the first awakening with her words and then decades later giving me a homeland, and finally for Elizabeth Clementson and Robert Lasner at Ig Publishing for taking a chance and believing in this book. And last but never least, to Scott Henderson for the spaces in between, the commas, with love.